Robert Jones Griffiths

**In Secret Places**

A Novel: Vol.III.

Robert Jones Griffiths

**In Secret Places**
*A Novel: Vol.III.*

ISBN/EAN: 9783337065423

Printed in Europe, USA, Canada, Australia, Japan

Cover: Foto ©Andreas Hilbeck / pixelio.de

More available books at **www.hansebooks.com**

# IN SECRET PLACES.

## A Novel.

BY

ROBERT J. GRIFFITHS, LL.D.

*IN THREE VOLUMES.*

VOL. III.

London:

SAMUEL TINSLEY,

10, SOUTHAMPTON STREET, STRAND.

1874.

# CONTENTS.

# IN SECRET PLACES.

## CHAPTER I.

### THE LAST WORDS.

ANNIE was still kneeling at the bedside, clasping the cold hands of her brother. During those minutes when they had been left alone he had told her everything concerning his fall,—how he had been led on by Emmerson from bad to worse, and how he suspected, nay, was certain, that this man was Mrs. Montressor's ally in some deep scheme of villany. He told her, also, how he had been received and treated kindly by the Druids, and how the stranger had endeavoured to soothe and comfort him.

"He is a strange man, and has immense power in the hills," he said. "Even Mrs. Montressor may feel its weight before long."

And Annie told him of her own sorrows, and of Mrs. Montressor's attempt to force her into a hateful marriage; an attempt which could, of course, never again be repeated. She said nothing of Frederick's engagement to Maria; and her brother therefore hoped that the estrangement would be but temporary. Then she spoke to him of that future world to which he was hurrying, and upon the borders of which he even then stood,—spoke with an earnestness which only a sister can feel when her only brother is on the verge of the unknown and untried sea of eternity which washes the confines of time. He listened as one in a dream—as one whose life-spring the chilling breath of Death had already touched.

"It is a glorious place," she said, in a low, murmuring voice; "but its glory is the presence of the Saviour and of God.

He can pardon you, my brother, if you ask Him."

It was a simple faith, and based on no idle dreams of philosophy, but it found its way to her listener's heart.

"I have asked Him, Annie, many times," he whispered, with a sob; "many a night when I was alone here I have asked Him for mercy."

"And He is very merciful to His erring children," said the poor child of sorrow, "and He will hear you, my brother."

Frederick and his companion returned to the cave, and Edward beckoned the former to his side.

"If I had listened to your counsels, Mr. Danvers, I might have died in a different place and in a happier manner," he said; "but that is over now. One thing grieves me; it is that I must leave my sister behind. In coming years I might have been a comfort instead of a curse to her; but that can never be now, and so I leave her to your care. Take her by the hand."

" But——" began Annie, remembering her brother's ignorance of Frederick's engagement.

" Do not speak, Annie," said her brother, raising himself on the pillow; " take her by the hand, Mr. Danvers;" and Frederick, hardly conscious of his own actions, did so.

" Promise that you will never lose sight of her—never forsake her—and that if ever she needs a friend you will help her," he said, with increasing excitement.

There was a moment's silence, and then, in a voice broken with conflicting emotions, Frederick said :—

" I promise, as God is my help ! "

Annie's face was buried in her hands, and her brother fell back exhausted. The last scene of all was not far distant now. Poor, erring sinner, he had wandered far from the great Father's fold, but at such a moment no one could cast a stone against him. Better to die thus, confessing one's sins, and to sink out of sight into the shadows of the grave, than to close a life of Pharisaical self-righteousness, only to find on the threshold of eternity, if it had never been discovered before, that self-virtue is the most damning of all human shams. Better to rest as a repentant prodigal in a rustic but peaceful Welsh village grave than beneath the lying marble of our cities.

Weep on, poor sister! as another soul seeks the noblest gift of God to man—the Life which springs from Death when the spirit begins to live as it explores heaven after heaven, and world after world, in God's boundless domains. Weep on, as the children of the earth must ever mourn when our weak humanity contemplates Death—this grim necessity of life. To us the stiffening limbs and the cold sweat of death, the eyes dimmed with the mists of the dark stream which flows around us and separates us from the regions beyond, are but a token that a dear one is leaving us for ever! Our eyes cannot pierce the veil which conceals from view the new suns and the new glories which blaze around the liberated soul as it wings its flight into the far regions of immortality. Her gaze could not follow that brother's spirit as it passed through the brief portals of Death, to rise into the glad sunshine of Life—life and beauty and golden sunlight, which greets every poor wanderer home— the home of ideal beauty and sweetness, or she would have dried her unavailing tears, in the full assurance that in all this fair world of ours there is nothing so blessed as the spectre which opens the gates of Immortality!

\*      \*      \*      \*      \*

Frederick led the almost broken-hearted girl away from the cave, and they stood once more beneath the twinkling stars. Through those silent heavens, perhaps, her brother's soul was winging its flight to its resting-place; and for a moment the three stood in silent thought, broken only by Annie's low weeping.

" Listen," said the Unknown, suddenly, in an impressive whisper.

A burst of solemn spirit-stirring music seemed to pervade the air with harmony; it rolled onwards and upwards until the air seemed full of exquisite melody. Anon it would almost die away in long-drawn notes, and then swell again with triumphant strains.

" The sages and fathers of our race are welcoming him to the land of the blest!" said the stranger, impressively; "through the dazzling halls of light they will lead him to his appointed place in the sacred home of eternal wisdom!"

But Annie could bear it no longer.

" Take me home," she whispered to Frederick; and, bidding the stranger farewell, they wended their way back again to the road.

But little was spoken on either side, for their hearts were too full for words; and yet Frederick would have given all he possessed in the world for the sake of holding her for one moment in his arms, and of pressing one kiss upon her lips. He could ask her for no explanation, for love is nothing unless it is trustful, and if she had sinned against their love, had not he done so also? And yet this dream of the past, which he believed had been for ever crushed out from his heart, revived with tenfold force at that moment when by every tie of honour he was bound to another—it swept over his soul with a bitterness which was painful indeed, and when at last he wished her a formal good-night, and left her to brood over her sorrows in the solitude of the Glyn, he would have given the best years of his life to have once more the right of comforting her. Oh God! in all the woes of life Thou hast none so bitter to impose upon men as the agony and despair of loving in vain!

The body was brought home the next day, and every one throughout the village attended Edward Hughes's funeral. Spiteful and harsh as many of them had been to the young man when alive, his faults were forgotten in his death. The grave is a wonderful reconciler—a strange healer of

differences. In the little churchyard by the
sea-side they laid the prodigal to rest, and
many a villager mingled his tears with
those of his sorrowing sister, as the stones
and earth fell thick and fast upon his coffin.
Throughout the whole assembly, indeed,
there was not one dry eye, and Mr. Campbell's voice was hoarse with emotion as he
read the funeral service.

" Yet, O Lord God most holy, O Lord
most mighty, O holy and most merciful
Saviour, deliver us not into the bitter pains
of eternal death."

The vicar's voice was earnestly pleading
as he read these touching words; and,
simple Protestants as they were, many a
prayer for mercy for the young man who lay
dead in his coffin went up from their hearts.

Frederick and the vicar wended their way
back together, almost in silence, and Annie
returned to the home that would never more
resound with her brother's voice. Dead
hopes—dead memories—dead joys—how
full of death is this world of life !

.

# CHAPTER II.

### A HILL-SIDE CONFERENCE.

EDWARD HUGHES and his failings were
buried in the tomb, and Mrs. Montressor
felt that her hold upon Annie was gone.
Of course she regretted this, for she was
never so happy as when she had a fellow-
creature in her power; but now that Frederick was pledged to marry her daughter,
she hoped and believed that this change in
the position of affairs, this one weapon the
less in her armoury, would not be of very
great importance.

Annie did not communicate with the
woman who had so nearly blighted her
life's happiness—she simply wrote to Mr.
Darby, informing him, as gently as she

could, that their engagement was at an end, an announcement which drove the reverend gentleman into despair. In vain he sought aid and counsel in the rich stores of philosophy which he had accumulated, for he found, like others before and after, that philosophy avails nothing to still the weary beatings of an aching heart. Poor man! with all his little eccentricities, he had loved Annie fondly and sincerely, in his own way, and to lose her was no slight blow to him.

Frederick spent the first few days after the funeral in a state of continual and feverish restlessness. The girl who alone had touched his heart, and whose love had been such a priceless treasure to him, in those days which were not very remote, but which seemed to be separated from the present by a great gulf of pain and mental suffering, that girl was free to listen again to the promptings of her own heart, and he was bound hand and foot to marry one whom, if he did not dislike her, at least he

did not love. It was a painful situation—
more deeply painful than any other he had
ever been in; and he could not dare to
approach the Glyn, nor could he bear to
visit Montressor House. The cairns had
never been visited, and probably never
would be, for he had more serious thoughts
to occupy his mind than to listen to the
learned lore of a lackadaisical young lady
above the resting-place of dead men's
bones; for the greatest achievements of
the past pale in our minds before the
realities of the present.

Maria was not disposed to be very exact-
ing towards her bridegroom elect, and, in
the peculiar state of the case, it was well
that her disposition was so accommoda-
ting; but still she could not but regard
his lengthy absence from the house with
alarm. Mr. Darby had duly informed her
mother of his dismissal from Annie's favour,
and Maria dreaded that Frederick would
again find his way to the farmhouse in the
valley. She determined, therefore, upon

sending him a formal invitation to dinner
one evening; but when the missive reached
the Lodge, its master had set out for a
ramble on the hills. No answer, therefore,
was returned to the young lady's note, and
as the truant did not make his appearance,
she was seriously alarmed. Frederick was
weary of wandering around his own grounds,
and he had therefore set out on this afternoon with the intention of enjoying a long
ramble on the hills; and he hoped that he
might see his mysterious friend the Druid.

He therefore bent his steps in the direction of that huge mass of rock, in the interior of which Edward's last breath had
been drawn. When he was once in the
midst of the rocks and the heather, and he
had left the road far behind, he had no
difficulty in discerning the particular one
of which he was in quest. It stood out
against the sky like a petrified giant, and
its dark shadow fell upon the wealth of
mountain verdure which clustered around
its base. The home of this mysterious

people was truly a stronghold, and, gazing
upon it, he thought how secure it was, for
no one would have dreamt that within that
apparently solid mass of stone there was a
settlement of living people.

He wandered round the rock, but was
unable to find any means of ingress. He
could not remember how they had entered
when accompanied by Sian, for the night
was so dark, and his thoughts were so full
of his strange and novel position, that he
had failed to observe how they had found
an entry into the apparently impenetrable
mass. He had been under the impression
that there was an opening in the rock, but
now, with the broad daylight to help him,
he could distinguish nothing of the kind.

He turned away disappointed, after a
time, and his eyes fell immediately upon a
figure which he recognised, seated in a
roughly-hewn seat in a small rock, at a little
distance from him. It was the stranger
whom he wished to see, and he made his
way up to him at once. His arms were

folded, and he was apparently lost in deep meditation ; but Frederick wondered how he came to be seated there so suddenly and silently, for he was certainly not there when Frederick had passed the spot a few minutes before.

"You were trying to unravel the mystery of our mountain home," said the Unknown, with a tinge of reproach in his voice; "striving to penetrate the secrets of a people whose faith you despise, but whose habits of life charm you by their very mystery."

"You are wrong," said Frederick, warmly; "my object was merely to find you out. I had half hoped to see you at the funeral of our friend."

"The children of the mountain never mingle with the faithless votaries of luxury and pleasure," was the calm reply; "the stream which has poured its crystal waters for untold ages through its mountain-bed, does not mingle with the muddy brooklet of yesterday. It is not very long ago when the village before us was not in existence, and when every inch of soil, from here to the sea, was cultivated by men who knew nothing of English vices and English follies. It is not so now. The purity of the Kymry is but little more than a memory of the past to-day, and we, who yet cling to what you will call an exploded superstition, cannot trust ourselves in the midst of the muddy tide."

" Then you deprecate the coming of the English into Wales at all? At least, you should remember that most of the comforts of life which the Welsh enjoy at present are owing to English civilization."

"True, you have taught them to steep their brains in drink; to swindle one another; to spend more money, and when they are not paid sufficiently, to refuse to work at all; to be lazy, litigious, and corrupt; to indulge in every extravagance which can possibly be suggested; and you have nearly succeeded in obliterating every national characteristic of our race. And what have you to offer in return? Nothing but sin, and evil, and misery. In all the dark history of the Kymry, the darkest, saddest day of all was that upon which our last brave prince died through treachery, and we became an English province."

"Is this a lament because of the decay of your religion, in consequence of English influence?" asked Frederick.

"Our religion was decaying before Edward the First's hordes ever trampled the greensward of my country," he replied; "and it would have dwindled away in the numbers of its followers in any case. We appeal only to the wise, and the truly wise in this world are very few indeed. They are all either Druids or else men who, knowing nothing of our primitive faith, have repudiated all other religions, and endeavoured to frame for themselves a great religion of Nature. You have men amongst you who are Druids in reality, although they would laugh at the name itself—men who are weary of the shams of every orthodox creed, and who strive to see the

Creator where alone He is to be found— in
the great empire of Nature."

"But surely, if you refuse to accept every
religious system which flourishes amongst
us, however well supported by evidence it
may be, you must have something definite,
some series of truths to propose as a substi-
tute?"

"You are wrong; Druidism is not a
formulated religion; it is the study of
Nature, and nothing more. We have but
few mysteries to impose upon man's credulity. We do not create our God and then
eat Him, as some of your enthusiasts do;
we do not attire a man in absurd finery,
call him a priest, and imagine that he is
invested with powers and gifts denied to
other men ; we do not assert that every one
who refuses to think as we do is to be
roasted in some unknown place of torment,
when he has left this world; or if he has
attended the building which you call a
church a certain number of times, and
contributed largely to the support of your

ministers, that he will be admitted to a region of bliss,—but bliss of which you yourselves are rather doubtful as to its nature! Our heaven is not a mere fabled abode like yours."

"So I gathered from your remarks on the previous occasion upon which we met," observed Frederick; "but it appears to me that to lay down positively and definitely the nature of the happiness of heaven—for we may as well call this country heaven— it is a name and nothing more—is a weak point in any religion. It is enough to hold out the motive afforded by a certainty of future bliss or woe. Mahomet's Koran is half full of details of heaven, which are simply ridiculous to every one who is not a sensual and profligate man; but we, as Christians, are sure of this, that whatever the delights of heaven may be, they are at least *pure* in their nature."

"We do not enter into minute details of the bliss to be enjoyed by the liberated soul," observed the Unknown, who had listened to Frederick's objection with perfect patience and composure. "We merely teach that heaven is a reproduction of the earth, or, more truly speaking, that the earth is a small and imperfect model of heaven; that everything which is beautiful here is to be found there in a state of perfection; and that everything which disfigures the earth has crept in by accident, or is a deviation from the original design; and that as our mission here is the study and contemplation of nature, so our happiness hereafter will mainly consist in sitting at the feet of the sages of old as they unravel the problems and the mysteries which have baffled us here."

"And yet, though you make the study of science to be the beginning and end of your religion, you are bitterly opposed to that civilization without which science would never have existed. Strange inconsistency!"

"Strange blindness!" was the reply. "Your boasted science is but in its infancy,

and has as yet but grasped the veriest rudi-
ments which were known to us thousands of
years ago. The man of science with you is
one who can talk glibly of a few scientific
facts for the amusement of fashionable
idlers, and who imagines that he has reached
the inner temple when he is yet hardly on
the threshold. The true student of nature
does not parade his knowledge before men,
for his life has a nobler object in view than
to please the ignorant multitude. Civilization has done nothing more than to endeavour to drag down science from its own
lofty pedestal."

"Then, for all your hatred for the world,
you have been in the haunts of men?"

"Yes, I have stood beneath the domes of
your temples, and spoken to your greatest
philosophers," he replied. "I have tra-
velled in foreign lands, and saw what a
terrible engine for enslaving the mind Christianity is, and I returned to my mountain
cave more confirmed in my faith than when
I left it. Science, which is as yet in its

infancy amongst hothouse philosophers, is a
giant amongst the despised followers of our
religion, and we can afford to bear the
odium of the ignorant, conscious, as we are,
that we shall live when they have passed
away."

"Have you, then, discovered the elixir of
life?" asked Frederick, with a slight sneer;
for, to assert this, would have been to his
mind a confession of imposture.

"I cannot reveal to you, an unbeliever,
the secrets of our religion—secrets of priceless value," was the calm and grave reply,
which had no trace of charlatanism about
it; "but the elixir of life, the magic liquid
of the alchemists, was a hopeless dream.  If
there be means of overcoming death, they
do not consist in nostrums like this.  But
we will not speak of a subject which you
cannot understand; but, as one of your own
writers has said, 'there is more in heaven
and earth than is dreamt of in your philosophy!'"

"This is undoubtedly true; but it appears

to me that your creed is a very unpractical
one."

"So is everything calculated to elevate
the world, to a casual observer; it is a mere
dream, and nothing more; but I do not
wish to convert you to my views, but I can
give you some proofs of my power."

"I do not wish to see them," replied
Frederick; "my mind has long been perplexed by religious disputes, and I am
weary of them."

"Spoken like a man who has no real love
for the truth; but the proofs I mentioned
are ones which concern you personally. I
could read in the maiden's face who accompanied you to her brother's death-bed the
whole history of your love, and the disappointment it brought. I know, and you
do not, the cause which led to her renuncia-
tion of you."

"What was it?" demanded Frederick,
eagerly.

"I dare not tell you yet," was the firm
reply; "you will learn it in time; but this

I wish to say, if your engagement with Miss Montressor should be broken by means beyond your control,—if the maiden you love be restored to your arms, and the sufferings of her brother be avenged,—and if these things are done by my instrumentality,—I, the poor outcast votary of an almost extinct and vanished creed, will you admit my power?"

"If these things can be done I will indeed believe in your power," he replied.

"Be it so; and, for the present, I must bid you adieu," he said, with a sudden solemnity; "the evening has come, and I must commune with the great Spirit. Farewell."

He rose, and walked slowly away, until he was lost to sight, and Frederick made the best of his way homewards. He found Maria's note on his table, and he despatched a servant with a message of apology; and then he sat down in his study to think over the words of the Unknown.

He did not derive much comfort from

them. He had not the least taint of superstitious weakness in his character, and
everything which in any way savoured of
mystery or credulity repulsed and dis-
pleased him. Calm, grave, and collected
as the Druid was,—a man evidently im-
bued with the creed which he professed,
he could not bring himself to place any
reliance upon his promises. If ever he
was to escape from the position into which
his own carelessness and wounded vanity
had brought him, it must be, he believed,
through his own exertions, and he set himself once more to endeavour to solve the
weary problem of his life. If half his
wealth would have satisfied her—if that
would induce her to set him free, he would
willingly have given it; but how could he
make such a proposal? It was absurd and
impracticable ; and as for an action for
breach of promise, his soul shrank from
the idea. He might have exclaimed, with
Francis I., at Pavia, "All is lost except
honour ; " but in his case the remark

would have been much more truthful than
on the lips of that erratic French monarch.
He had lost the sweetest hope of his life—
the brightness which had entered his heart
had all faded away; a prospect of peace
and happiness in the future had vanished,
and given way to dark shadows and storm-
clouds, and Frederick's heart was very
heavy. Woman's love! how sweetly dangerous a thing it is, when a pair of white
arms, tresses of sunny brown hair, and
deep blue eyes, can wreck a man's happiness for life. *Vanitas vanitatum*—the old,
old story!

## CHAPTER III.

### MR. DARBY IS REPENTANT.

THE Glyn was at peace again. The tread
of many feet which had been heard in its
ancient faded rooms when the last son of
the family was carried to his long resting-
place was heard no longer; the sympathiz-
ing relations, of whom there were many,—for
it is astonishing how intricately Welsh people are related to one another—had gone,
and the house had undergone a thorough
cleansing, for Annie, like all her fair
countrywomen, had a horror of dirt. Everything which had belonged to her brother
was reverently and carefully treasured up
and preserved, and a simple tombstone
was placed over his grave. Every Sunday

morning, as she went to church to superintend the Sunday School, which generally
consisted of about three sleepy boys, and
perhaps one or two women, when the
weather and their inclinations permitted
them to come, Annie would place fresh
wreaths of flowers on the stone, with a
kind of vague though unconfessed idea
that she was doing something to please
her brother.   She was not, perhaps, a
Protestant, in the extreme sense of the
word, though in that far and remote place
they knew but little of the keen contro-
versies of the day; but this tribute of
flowers was one she never failed to pay;
and, perhaps, as she knelt at night, to
send up her evening petitions to heaven,
there might have been a mention of her
dead brother's name.   It might have been
wrong, but it may have been none the less
efficacious.   At any rate, a prayer from a
simple maiden's lips is more likely to be
heard than those of all the white-robed
and mitred priests of the world.

She had not yet succeeded in shaking
off her illness, and her cheeks had not
recovered their wonted bloom, but she
persisted in attending to her own particular duties. Her garden, upon which she
prided herself, had to be cared for, and
latterly it had been very much neglected.
The old women, too, who lived in the
cottages around, had much to confide to
her, — complaints about rheumatism and
sleepless nights, and other infirmities peculiar to old ladies; and to all these endless
narrations of real and imaginary evils she
listened kindly and sympathizingly. The
old dames were unanimous in their delight
that their youthful mistress was not to be
married, and especially to Mr. Darby, whom
they all disliked, although none of them had
ever seen him, but they had an idea that
the young lady disliked him, and, of course,
she must be right. Matrimony, according
to them, was nothing but a snare and a
delusion, and they were rejoiced to find,
they said, that she had escaped the pitfall.

Nearly every house in the neighbourhood, too, had to be visited, and the wants
of many a poor woman were relieved. The
singing meetings in the sea-side church—
for they were held aloof from Glynarth,
although Mr. Campbell officiated in both
places—on Thursday evenings had fallen
into oblivion, and had to be revived. It
was usually a very small one, for not more
than half-a-dozen people, mostly women,
attended; and their knowledge of music
was extremely small, and their voices not
very tuneful. They came there, in fact,
because it was a way of passing the evening—a little more pleasant, perhaps, than
falling asleep by the fire.

But to their young instructress these
meetings were a much more serious business. She considered it to be an important
part of her mission in the world to cultivate the rather unpromising intellectual soil
around her, and she devoted herself assidu-
ously to the task. There was no one in the
parish to dispute her will. Mr. Campbell

might be somebody at Glynarth, but there
he was nothing when once he had doffed his
surplice—Annie was supreme and omnipo-
tent.

And so the singing classes were in a
short time in full swing, and the school on
Sunday mornings flourished in everything
except in numbers, and the service on Sunday afternoons was so attractive that many
of the villagers from Glynarth came down
as an after dinner walk, a rather enjoyable combination of pleasure and devotion.
Frederick, however, never came, although
sometimes she half-hoped, half-dreaded to
see him. He kept aloof because he could
not bear to see her; and as she frequently
came up to Glynarth church on Sunday
evenings, he abstained altogether from
going there, much to Mr. Campbell's
horror; but no amount of ecclesiastical re-
monstrance would induce him to change
his determination.

He, as well as every one else in Glynarth,
heard of her rejection of the minister, and

the tidings produced a mingled sensation of
pleasure and pain.    The next intelligence
that he received concerning her was that
she had been taken ill again.

She had recommenced her duties too suddenly, and endeavoured to do more than
her strength would permit, and she had to
give way at last.    She had been in Glynarth
one evening, visiting some friends and rela-
tives, and she was seized with faintness and
dizziness, which however passed away in a
few hours, and she set out for the Glyn un-
accompanied.    On the way—and it was a
dark, secluded road, overshadowed by trees
—she felt her strength leaving her again,
when just at this moment Mr. Darby presented himself.    He had been rehearsing a
discourse on the banks of the river, and had
made his way into the road for the purpose
of going home.

"You are unwell, Miss Hughes," he said,
deferentially, and even humbly; "allow me
to offer you my arm."

"Thank you; but I am not very far from

home," she said, faintly, for there were too many unpleasant reminiscences connected with the minister to make his presence agreeable to her.

"It is nearly a mile off, and really you are not at all well," he said, earnestly. "I hope it is because of no prejudice against me that you refuse my help. You have sufficient reason in the past to dislike me, but let the past be forgotten."

He drew her hand through his arm, and then walked slowly down the valley.

"I have wished for an opportunity to speak to you," he said, in the same humble voice, "to tell you how deeply sorry I am that I ever lent myself to Mrs. Montressor's scheme against you. I loved you deeply, but not with the true love that you ought to inspire, for the essence of real love is a forgetfulness of self, and my love was very selfish."

"We will not speak of it," she said, gently.

"But I must speak of it," he persisted. "After all the suffering you have endured

on my account, it is only right and just that
I should make the fullest reparation in my
power—and that is not much.   When Mrs.
Montressor first told me that she could induce you to marry me, I confess that I
welcomed the promise with joy, for I could
not foresee the intense pain it would entail
upon you.   Pardon me if I thought that
woman's love was by no means enduring,
and that it would not cause very much incon-
venience or trouble to you.   I have discovered my mistake since then, and I
deplore it most deeply."

"Let us forget it all, Mr. Darby," she
said, in a low voice ; "I can readily forgive
you for all your real and fancied offences
against me."

"It is impossible to forget these things,"
he answered ; "but I am striving to make
some atonement for them.   What has often
puzzled me is, how this woman could ever
have induced you to fall in with her views."

"She threatened that unless I did so she
could hang my brother—my dead brother—

if she chose.    It was utterly false, but I
feared then that it was true," she said.

Edward had simply told her that Mrs.
Montressor's accusation was unfounded, that
he had confided the full history of the transaction on the mountain to the Unknown
alone.    The dying youth was not even
aware of Emmerson's marriage to Mrs.
Montressor, or else possibly he might have
revealed a little of that individual's history.
As it was, the grave had closed over the
secret,—at least Emmerson sincerely hoped
so.

"Poor child!  I little dreamt of this,"
said the minister ; " what a desperate woman
she must be.   Of course, I never imagined
that she had recourse to actual threats,
or else things might have been rather
different."

They had reached the gateway; and
Annie, who felt very unwell, was anxious to
enter, but Mr. Darby detained her for one
moment.

" Say that you forgive me fully and completely," he said, pleadingly, " and that you will not hate me in the future as you have had reason to do in the past."

"I have never *hated* you—indeed I have not," she said; " and if my forgiveness is worth anything, you have it, Mr. Darby. Good-night, and I thank you for your great kindness."

She really liked him after his frank confession, or rather, she did not dislike him as she had done before. And he, poor man, walked homewards with very conflicting feelings. He had lost her for ever, and he was a man although a philosopher also, and the loss affected him keenly. He had made this apology because he had determined for the future to act honourably in the matter, and he felt somewhat indignant, because Mrs. Montressor had evidently used him as a catspaw in order to get rid of Annie.

He reached home in a state of deep dejection, and drew off his overcoat slowly and thoughtfully.

" I have nothing of hers as a keepsake,"

he mused, " nothing upon which her hand
has rested—except the sleeve of this coat.
Let me see."

He brought forth a pair of scissors and
cut off the sleeve, to be treasured ever
afterwards as a relic of her. Philosophers
do strange things sometimes; and Solomon,
great sage as he was, was a simpleton when
women were concerned. " Only a woman's
hair," wrote the grim old Dean; and a
tress of sunny brown hair, cut half laughingly half seriously at the Glyn one evening,
was Frederick's chief solace in life. But
the sleeve of a coat! Other men with
lesser minds would have laughed at the
absurdity, but Mr. Darby was a philosopher, and he treasured it as a memento of
the girl he had lost.

## CHAPTER IV.

### " LOVE CANNOT DIE."

THOSE days of restless longing for the seemingly unattainable—days of weary struggling against the inevitable, were not without their effect upon Frederick. Many times a day he felt a strong, wild desire to go down to the Glyn; to hear the loved voice once more, even although a barrier had been for ever raised between them, and as often he would strive to stifle a love which society would regard as dishonourable.

One evening, however, he could endure the strong mental conflict no longer, and he set out in that direction which he had not traversed since the day when Edward's body was carried to the grave. He had waited until the twilight hour, when few people would be abroad, and he wished only to see the house which was the home of his heart's idol; to watch, perhaps, the flickering light of the candle by which she was reading or working—working at the everlasting embroidery—as it cast its rays upon the window-blind, and threw its shadows on the garden and grass-plots without. He would not dare to enter, for he had now no right to take the drooping maiden in his arms, and to comfort the lonely and aching heart. He could only stand afar off and witness the solitude of a life which he would have given worlds to brighten and cheer, could he have done so.

The road was nearly deserted. A few weary labourers met him on their way home, and exchanged kindly greetings with him, but this was only near the village. Farther on, as he descended into the valley, there was no one to interrupt his gloomy reveries; and when at last he stood before

the house, no one came to interfere with
his vigil.

The light from the parlour, where she
usually sat, was weak and uncertain, and
evidently came from the fire alone.  Every
other room in the house was quite dark, and
the old women had gone to bed at a very
early hour, as was their wont; for they
never burned candles and peat to enable
them to sit up when they had nothing whatever to do.  And so, with no companion
but his own misery, he stood there and
watched.

An hour perhaps had passed away, when
he saw the door gently open, and a girlish
form which he knew well stole out.  She
was closely muffled up, and seemed to move
with caution and even timidity, for she cast
a hurried, nervous glance around, as if
to discover whether she was observed.
She could not see the dark form of a man,
which stood in the deep shadow of a
friendly tree, and she opened the iron gate
carefully and almost noiselessly, and passed

out into the road.   Then she bent her steps
rapidly in the direction of the sea, and
Frederick followed her at a little distance.

She hurried quickly through the little
village, which was near her home, and then
the road became still darker and gloomier,
for it was shaded by trees planted closely
together, and the river flowed upon the
other side.   Once she paused, fancying that
she heard footsteps following her; but as
all was still, she again renewed her journey.

For some days she had been very weak
and ill, and throughout the whole of this
day she had been unusually unhappy and
depressed.   She had, however, refused to
receive a doctor, and her ancient attendants,
who knew nothing of the nature of her
disease, gave her up at last, recommending
some warm milk-posset before she went
to bed—advice which, like most other well-
meant counsels in this world, was not taken.
And now she had come out with a strange
desire in her breast, and in a state of mind
almost approaching to delirium.   The silence

and loneliness of her home were insupportable to her, and she was going to seek a remedy in a place of still greater loneliness and gloom—the churchyard!

She walked rapidly onwards until she came to that sacred resting-place of the dead, on the beautiful shore of the Cardigan Bay. The gate was locked, but she had the key, and, before Frederick could discover where she had gone, she was within the enclosure, and was threading her way to the grave of her dear ones; but when he saw the un-locked portal, in which the key still re-mained, the whole purpose of that secret visit flashed into his mind.

He had no superstitious dread of goblins and corpse-candles, and a thousand grim visitants from the other world would not have kept him from her side at that moment. He entered the churchyard, and made his way also in the direction which she had just taken before him; and the darkness, which was now very dense, and unlighted almost by a single star, prevented her from seeing him, as he came noiselessly towards her over the soft turf.

She was lying upon the grave, with her face buried in the flowers, which she herself had planted there; and, as he stood hesitating whether he could intrude upon the sacredness of her grief, she spoke in a low, broken voice:

"Father, mother, brother, and lover— they are all gone from me," she moaned. "Oh! that my heart, too, would cease its beatings, and be at rest! What have I done, that I alone should hunger for love —that I alone should break my heart? My love—my love!"

He could not listen unmoved to that plaintive, despairing voice, and, raising the astonished girl in his arms, he pressed her to his heart.

"I am here, my darling," he said, in a low, tender voice; "here to comfort and to protect you. Good heavens! how much you must have suffered!"

This last exclamation rose to his lips as

he saw how wan and pallid her face was,
how unlike her former self she had become.
Suffering and pain, keen and intense, were
depicted in every feature—in the very tones
of her voice.

"I have suffered a great deal," she said,
endeavouring to withdraw from his embrace,
"but it will soon be over now, I trust.  Mr.
Danvers, you must leave me.  We must
not remain thus."

"And why not?"  he asked, almost pas-
sionately; "is it so easy to trample on the
purest feelings of the heart, and to forget for
ever the sweetest moments of my life?  Do
you think that I am changed, my darling?"

"You are engaged to Miss Montressor,"
she said, in a low voice.

"And you were engaged to the minister,"
he retorted.  "Engagements are made every
day, with which love has nothing whatever
to do, and both these cases are examples
in point; but if I were free again, Annie;
if I had nothing to fetter me, and again
came to you, what would your answer be?"

"Do not ask me," she pleaded; "it is cruel to torture me thus."

"What would your answer be, my own?" he said, in a still softer and tenderer voice; "is the old love completely forgotten? Am I banished from your heart for ever? Do you still love me, Annie?"

She was weeping softly on his breast, and made no reply in words, but he could perceive that she was trembling violently.

"The bitterest moments in all my life have been those when I thought that you were lost to me for ever," he went on; "and now the delight of holding you in my arms again is not altogether unmixed with pain—with dread lest I should lose you again. Must we part, Annie?"

"No, no!" she whispered; and what his response was it is impossible to say, for there was silence for some minutes— silence, so far as words were concerned, but full of eloquence to the two miserably-happy beings who had just been re-united.

The situation was certainly rather a romantic one. He was seated on a grave-stone, and Annie lay in his arms. Not thirty yards away the sea was moaning and dashing against the shore, and there was hardly a light to be seen anywhere. In addition to these circumstances, the night was rather cold, and, in Annie's state of health, it was decidedly dangerous to linger there; but when were lovers afraid of taking cold?

"I cannot live without you, my darling," he went on, in a low, fervent voice; "everything has conspired to throw obstacles in the way of our love, and perhaps I myself have been weak and yielding too, but I cannot stifle my love, and if the whole world tried to sever us, we will come together again, my own. And in the dark days, that we will hope are passed and gone, you have suffered too, dearest."

"Suffered! oh, yes," she responded, wearily; "first I lost you, and then I was nearly forced to marry a man I could never love. Then came Edward's death, and one after another I saw every one and everything which was dear to me taken away. There has been nothing in my life hitherto but sorrow and trouble."

"Nothing but our love, dearest," he whispered; "it drives away the darkness and beautifies everything. To hold you in my arms once more—to look into your dear face is all that is needed to make life happy."

"And Miss Montressor?" she asked, doubtfully.

"Between Miss Montressor and myself there has never been even a semblance of love," he answered, "not on my part, at least; and when I see her and tell her—as I will do at once—that I have loved you from the beginning, and that my love is stronger and firmer now than it has ever been, she must set me free."

"She will *not* set you free," said a deep, emphatic voice behind them, which, in the silence and desolation of that churchyard,

came with startling distinctness upon their
ears; "do not cherish vain hopes which
will never be realized."

It was the Unknown—the Druid of the
hills; but what motive had brought him to
that spot it was impossible to guess, and to
question him would have been useless. He
stood there with, a long, black mantle
wrapped closely around him, and a slouched
hat upon his head half concealed his features.

"You will appeal to Miss Montressor's
generosity, and to her sense of right, and
you will appeal in vain," he went on;
" and this very step is the surest which you
can take to raise an insurmountable barrier
between yourself and the maiden you love.
If you wish never to see her again—never
more to hear the voice which is sweeter to
your soul than all earthly music—you will
go to Miss Montressor to-morrow and plead
for your freedom."

Annie clung to her lover with alarm, for
the mystery which surrounded this man

filled her with dread, and in her weak state of health she was not able to bear great excitement.

"What must I do, then?" demanded Frederick. "As a man of honour I cannot renew my engagement with the girl I love whilst I am bound to another, and I cannot give Annie up. What *can* I do?"

"Must you act with *honour*, as you call it, towards those who have entrapped you into an engagement with one whom you care nothing for, and who probably cares nothing for you?" he asked. "Must you place those who are prepared to go any lengths, in order to gain their object, upon a level with others—with the good, and honourable, and pure? You have been deceived—entrapped; and most men would have discovered it ere this."

"Still, that is no reason why I should be a villain," replied Frederick; "if they have deceived me, I ought to inform them of the discovery of their plot, or else how can I disentangle myself from it?"

"Leave that to me, and to those who act under my control," observed the Unknown. "I can fathom their wickedness when other human eyes are blind to it, and I will punish it. Let events take their course, and in a very short time you will be free, and those who now reign in Montressor House will be—— I cannot tell you where."

Frederick and Annie were both silent, more with amazement than alarm, and the Druid went on :—

"You hear the ocean washing the shore," he said, waving his hand in the direction of the sea, which was only a few yards distant from them; "it is breaking down gradually the rocks which stem its progress—slowly perhaps, but very surely. And so the Eternal Justice, which rules the world, breaks down in time the strongest barriers which man's depravity can raise. It will be so with Mrs. Montressor. She has sinned deeply against human and Divine laws, and the avenger is very near at hand now."

"What has she done?" asked Annie,

with a slight. tinge of woman's natural curiosity.

"I cannot tell you now," he replied, drawing his mantle still closer around him, "but her course is nearly run; and if your lover wishes to save you from suffering and danger, he must not reveal his suspicions to the daughter of this evil—this falling house."

He went away as abruptly as he came, flitting like a shadow among the tombstones and through the gateway, and then Frederick thought it time to take Annie home.

"He may be right," he said, thoughtfully, as they walked away from the church; "there may be some deep scheme of villany in the case, but it would satisfy my conscience if I were to tell Miss Montressor of the true state of the case."

Annie was more timid and fearful, and dreaded Mrs. Montressor. She tried to persuade her lover to renounce his intention, and expressed her confidence in the Druid's power.

"He does not speak like a boaster," she

urged, "but with the calm assurance of sustained power. In any case it can do no harm to wait a little longer."

"It may do great harm," he replied, "for I cannot see that I ought to act dishonourably because others have done so. Besides, I have not much faith in a man who sur-. rounds himself with mystery, and deals only in hints and ominous suggestions. I prefer to trust to the dictates of common sense."

"But these Druids are wonderful people, as you will find," she persisted, "and he may be right after all. But do as you think best."

She thought not of the possible danger to herself at which the Unknown had hinted. If Frederick considered a certain course to be the best, she was quite ready to believe it to be so.

They parted, with an eager longing on his part for the time when he could again call her his own—and upon hers, with a feeling that she had been doing something wrong, or at least something from which future trouble would ensue, and she was right.

# CHAPTER V.

## FREDERICK IN A DILEMMA.

MARIA's life in the dingy, grand, but very dull manor-house was a monotonous one; and from the education she had received, she had no mental resources to fall back upon—nothing which could dispel the tediousness of that dull, dead time. Her father-in-law's society was inexpressibly distasteful to her, for she was certain that he had gained his ascendancy over her mother by means which would not bear examination, and his manners and conversation were more adapted to the stable and the village pothouse than for ears polite. Mr. Emmerson could indeed be entertaining and almost refined when he chose to exert him-

self, but that was not often; and a gulf
seemed to be fixed between him and his
step-daughter—a barrier which neither of
them were very anxious to remove. He
wished only to enjoy his pipe and an unlimited amount of drink, whilst Maria was
but too glad to be relieved of his society.

As for Mrs. Emmerson she had sunk into
a fretful and irritable state of mind, constantly dreading the appearance of Edmund
Montressor on the scene, and fearful lest
Frederick should succeed, after all her pains,
in eluding her grasp. Her health suffered
under the influence of her anxiety, and thus
Maria was left almost entirely to herself.

She also lived in a state of constant alarm
lest she should lose Frederick, but she was
not influenced by her mother's sordid and
mercenary motives. Brought up, as she
had been, amid circumstances not con-
ducive to the formation and growth of the
higher virtues, there was yet much that was
estimable in her character. Overawed at all
times by her mother's superior will and

greater strength of purpose, yet her mind
revolted with horror from the dark schemes
in which Mrs. Emmerson engaged, and she
really loved Frederick with a strong and
absorbing passion.    She was conscious that
this love was not mutual, and at the time
that she had proposed to him she did not
care for him as she did now—now that her
every hope in life was centred and bound up
in him.    She was indeed to be pitied, but
Frederick, although he might pity her,
could never love her, so that her prospects
were cheerless, and her hopes based upon a
very insecure foundation.

The morning after his interview with
Annie, Frederick set out for Montressor
House, with the intention of asking Maria
to release him from their engagement.    It
was a beautifully fine day, the sky being
almost cloudless, and there was a refreshing breeze from the hills.    It was almost
like a summer's day, and Frederick would
have been supremely happy but for the unpleasant errand upon which he was engaged

As it was he approached the house with something akin to the feelings of a criminal as he walks to the place of execution.

Maria was standing on the lawn, equipped in her riding-habit, as he came up, and either the freshness of the breeze, or else his approach—and perhaps both—gave her cheeks a heightened colour, which added to her handsome appearance. She was certainly a fine girl, and society would decide that she was by far more suitable to Frederick than the Welsh maiden whom he loved; but the grand passion very seldom regards the fitness of things, and, as he drew near, he could not help instituting a mental comparison between Annie and her who stood before him beneath the soft light of the morning sun, and the comparison was by no means favourable to Maria.

"And so you are still in Glynarth, sir," she said, with apparent gaiety, but still with a very perceptible amount of reproach in her voice. "I really thought that you had taken your departure."

"I have not been very well," he replied,
gravely; "and I have been very much
occupied with various matters, so that I
could not call. You are bent upon an
expedition, I see."

"Yes; I intend to ride over to the cairns
I spoke about," she said; "perhaps you
will accompany me," she added, timidly,
as if doubtful whether he would accept the
invitation.

"I shall be very pleased," he said; "but
I must send over to the Lodge for my horse.
Perhaps you will allow one of your servants
to go?"

A groom was despatched, and, until he
returned, they walked about the lawn, con-
versing on indifferent topics, but both were
labouring under a sense of restraint, as if
conscious of some subject which occupied
their minds, but which they were loth to
touch upon.

When the man returned they set out on
their journey, and neither of them spoke
much until they reached the spot consecrated

by the supposed tombs of ancient British
chieftains.   They consisted of small mounds
or barrows, and upon the summit of each
was a pile of large stones, where it was
supposed that the Druids had formerly celebrated their mystic rites, and that, when
Christianity had been introduced to the
country, these sites were selected as the
resting-places of heroes, because of the
veneration which the people, although
nominally Christians, still accorded to
them.   At an earlier period still, perhaps
when Druidism was prevalent everywhere
in Wales and in England also, these barrows, similar as they are in their formation
to many scattered over England, had been
constructed as burial-places; but in this particular spot the legend told only of chieftains
who had perished in a great border battle,
and had been buried here.   To an antiquarian
the matter would probably present itself in a
different light, but Maria and the dwellers
around were not antiquarians, and accepted
with implicit trust the common legend.

Frederick noticed that the place upon
which they stood was not very far removed
from the abode of the Druids, and he
wondered whether any unseen hearers were
listening to their conversation.

"You are not very cheerful this morning," said Maria, after an interval of
silence; "in fact, you have not spoken a
dozen sentences since we came out."

"No, that is because I came out this
morning with the intention of speaking to
you upon a very serious subject, and I
hardly know how to approach it," he said,
seizing this opportunity for broaching the
matter which oppressed his mind.

The colour upon her cheeks came and
went, as if she surmised the purport of his
thoughts; but she gave him no help; she
simply said, "What is it?"

"It is about our engagement," he said,
in some confusion; and then, as she turned
her face away, and remained silent, he went
on, "I have felt for some time past that, in
forming this engagement, I was entering

upon a course which could only result in unhappiness, if not absolute misery, to both of us,—an engagement which can have but one result, and that not a pleasant one."

"I do not quite understand you," she said, in a low voice.

"Perhaps not; it is difficult to explain myself without wounding your feelings," he pursued; but she interrupted him:

"Never mind my feelings," she said; "tell me exactly what you meant to say."

"I wished to explain that when our engagement was first formed I was placed in painful and peculiar circumstances," he went on, gathering fresh hope from her remark. "I ought not to conceal from you that I loved Annie Hughes with an affection which I could feel for no other woman; but at that time I believed that my love was a hopeless one. Things have changed since then, and I felt that it would be dishonourable on my part to conceal from you the state of my feelings. I loved her then, and I love her still; and it is

therefore better for both of us that our engagement should come to an end."

"Do not say so, Frederick," she said, in
a low, pleading voice, as she turned towards
him, and would have fallen at his feet, but
that he prevented her. "Do not take away
from me the only hope I have in life! This
girl can never love you as I love you; she
can never experience the bitter sorrow I
should feel if you were to leave me! Do
not take away the hope of becoming your
wife, and with it every ray of light in the
world!"

She burst into a flood of passionate tears,
which moved him in spite of himself. He
could bear everything better than the sight
of a fair woman weeping, and her grief,
evidently genuine as it was, was not without its effect upon him.

"But I can never love you, Miss Montressor," he said; "to continue this engagement would be to make Miss Hughes and
myself miserable; and surely you could
hardly accept a husband who you knew

loved another. It is a very painful position for both of us at the present moment, but it is nothing to the pain which will result in after years if you still hold me to my promise."

"I cannot release you—indeed I cannot," she murmured; "you are dearer to me than the whole world, and I cannot give you up."

There was no help for it—he saw in a moment that it would be useless to argue with her, and very reluctantly, therefore, he gave up the attempt.

"I am very sorry," he said, gravely and quietly, "and I hope that when you consider the matter quietly over you will arrive at a different conclusion. Will you mount your horse?"

He assisted her into the saddle, and then seated himself on his own steed. Antiquarian lore was completely forgotten, for the glories and wonders of past ages are obliterated by the smallest troubles of the present.

They rode homewards in silence. She

had drawn down her veil to conceal her features, and he was meditating anxiously upon his position, so that neither were inclined to converse. When he had escorted her home, and was about to turn away, she said, in a voice rendered indistinct by her tears:—

"Say that you did not mean half the cruel things you have spoken this morning."

"It would be very wrong and untrue were I to say so," he answered, firmly; "I was very much in earnest, and I am sorry that you differ from me as to what we ought to do."

She made no reply, but beckoned to a servant to take her horse, and then, with a scarcely audible "good-morning" she entered the house, and sought the privacy of her own room, where she gave full vent to her grief and despair.

They were both very real and genuine, for, as she had told him, she loved him as sincerely and strongly as a woman could love a man ; but this frank confession of his affection for her rival, instead of hopelessly discouraging her, after a time roused something of her mother's nature in her breast.

"Mamma must hear of this," she said, with flushed cheeks and a heaving breast; "this girl shall not carry off the prize, if we can prevent it—and we *must* prevent it, even if her death alone can put an end to his love."

As if death ever can put an end to love ! It is death that purifies and spiritualizes it, and almost renders earthly affection immortal.    Annie's death would be the greatest barrier which Maria could raise between Frederick Danvers and herself.

She sought her mother's apartments, and found her awaiting the post.

"You have been agitating yourself this morning," she said rather sharply, as her daughter entered; "something must be the matter.  I hope that it is no new trouble, for heaven knows I have enough to bear as it is."

" Yes, it is a new trouble, mamma," said Maria, wearily; "there seems to be nothing else in the world now," and she proceeded to narrate the conversation between herself and Frederick.

" This is a very serious matter," said her mother anxiously, when she had concluded; " evidently they have met, and perhaps she has told him of the threat by which I induced her to renounce him, and to consent to marry the minister. If she has done so, what must he think of us? "

" It will strengthen his determination to break off our engagement," replied her daughter; " but from the conversation this morning, I do not think that he is aware of it—indeed, I am sure of it; but he may be told of it at any moment."

" Not if the girl is removed," said her mother, significantly; " but in an affair of this kind you are of no use, Maria. Leave me now. I will think of it."

Maria was well content to leave the matter in her mother's hands, for, though lashed to fury by the supposed slight which had been put upon her, she shrank from entering into any scheme which could injure her rival. Others might do so if they chose, but she would remain ignorant of it, quite willing to reap the reward of the villany of others. Her tender heart would not permit her to hurt Annie; but if her mother did so, she would not object.

In the meantime Frederick was wending his way homewards, with a feeling of sore disappointment at his heart. He had hoped that Maria did not care very much for him, and that she would have readily freed him from an engagement which had become irksome, when he explained the state of the case to her; now that hope was gone, and he was sorely perplexed as to what his future course would be.

He entered his study, and drew forth from his desk a sheet of note-paper, on which he wrote a few lines to Annie.

"MY DEAREST ANNIE," he began, and then

it struck him that this mode of address was formal and cold, although he could find nothing more suitable, so that he allowed it to stand. "Miss Montressor has refused to release me, and, until something is decided, I must not see you. I am placed in a very unpleasant position, and can only wait in the hope that time may solve my difficulties.

Ever yours,

FREDERICK DANVERS."

"Unless my Druid friend fulfils his promise, it will be a long time before I write to her again," he thought, aloud.

"Your Druid friend will fulfil his promise," said the voice of the Unknown, who was standing at the open window; "but, by your rash conduct to-day, you have imperilled the safety of the maiden whom you profess to love."

He stepped uninvited into the room, and seated himself opposite to Frederick.

"You would not have treated Miss Mon-

tressor so tenderly if you knew of the misery
which her mother has brought upon Annie
Hughes," he said; "by the threat of hanging her brother—a threat which she knew
could never be carried out—she compelled
her to accept this Unitarian minister—the
foolish minister of a foolish creed, as all
your creeds are—as her future husband,
and, at the present moment, this woman is
plotting to remove her daughter's rival
to some place of security—security from
your attentions."

"How, in heaven's name, do you know
this?" asked Frederick, with great surprise.

"How do I know of that sweet conversation this morning?" was the sarcastic
rejoinder; "by means which you, with all
your boasted science, have lost. That is a
question which does not concern you; but,
as you have brought this girl into danger,
it is but fair that you should assist in pro-
tecting her."

"I will, with my heart's blood, if
necessary," he said, fervently.

" Good, and now I must bid you adieu;
when the moment for action comes I will
summon you."

Before Frederick could detain him he
passed out through the open window, and
was quickly lost to view.

# CHAPTER VI.

### THE UNKNOWN'S STORY.

FREDERICK's hopes had been thus rudely shattered. He was not disposed to inquire too minutely into the reality of Maria's love; but much as he despised her mother, much as he regretted the unfortunate entanglement into which he had been drawn, he was still inclined to believe in the reality of her love, and it gave him nothing but unmixed pain. Love is so rare in this world, notwithstanding all that has been written respecting it, that it is not heedlessly to be thrown away; and Maria's love was indeed a hopeless one.

He could not shut his eyes to the fact that Mrs. Emmerson had broken off the engage-

ment between Annie and himself; darker
deeds even than this had been broadly
hinted at by the Druid, and there was
nothing but hot indignation in his heart as
he thought of her, and nothing but regretful
pity as he thought of her daughter. She
had not sinned against him, unless, indeed,
the love which she bore him was a sin
against him; and yet he shrank from the
idea of a union with her.

He could see the result but too clearly.
Nurtured and educated as she had been
amongst the hills and valleys of Wales, she
regarded everything through the medium
of her own untutored passions, and the
Englishman who had, unfortunately for
both of them, entered the place, had been
elevated in her mind to a pedestal of
magnified heroism such as but few of the
most romantically inclined young ladies of
Belgravia assign to the objects of their
affections. He guessed as much, and knew
that it could not last; that marriage is
the gate through which dreaming lovers

return from heaven to this cold, practical
world again ; and that perhaps in a few
years, nay, even months, her love might be
changed to indifference—perhaps something
worse. And as for him—if he were married
a hundred times, the image of his first love
would never be obliterated from his mind—
a love which had interwoven itself with his
every thought, and had become a part of his
very existence.

And yet he saw no hope of release
consistent with his very strict sense of
honour. He could not accuse her mother
of crimes of which he knew not even their
nature, and of which he had not a particle
of proof; and anything short of this would
not shake off his fetters. For some days
he deliberated anxiously thus with himself,
and at length decided upon leaving Glynarth for the remainder of the three months
during which he was yet to be free, in the
hope that change of scene might revive
him, and that, during his absence, something
might occur to terminate his engagement.

His resolve became known in the village in a very short time, even before it reached Montressor House, and the Unknown, in his mountain castle, heard of it.

A week was necessary to prepare for his departure, and during that time he shut himself up in his own study, sometimes venturing to call at the House; but as Maria and her mother had remonstrated against this sudden step, he did not care to approach them too frequently. He therefore set to work to renew his acquaintance with his favourite classical authors, in the hope that steady occupation would lighten his anxieties. He was thus employed one evening, when the week had well-nigh dragged its weary length away. A bright fire blazed and crackled merrily on the hearth; the heavy curtains were closely drawn, and he sat at a reading-table, with cosy slippers on his feet, deeply engaged with Lucretius, when a ring at the outer bell caused him to raise his head and listen.

It was nearly ten o'clock, and hardly a

night for visitors, for a cold, heavy rain was pouring down in torrents, and the wind was strong enough to drive it into the clothing of every pedestrian who happened to be abroad. Ten o'clock, too, was a late hour for Glynarth, an hour when most of the villagers had retired to rest, or were warming themselves before expiring fires preparatory to doing so. And yet there was some one at the gate, some impatient individual, too; for another peal, louder and longer than the first, broke the stillness of the night in another minute or two.

A servant tapped at the door of the study, and Frederick commanded him to enter.

"A stranger, sir, wishes to see you," he said.

"A stranger! Who can he be?" asked his master.

"I cannot say, sir," replied the man; "he is muffled up, and does not look a very respectable person."

Frederick had an idea now as to who the

new comer was, and he directed the man to show him in. He did so; and the Druid—for it was he—was ushered into the room.

He stood in silence until the servant had closed the door, and then he said, as he cast aside his wrappers one after the other,—

"You did not expect to see me to-night?"

"No; it is certainly an unexpected pleasure," said Frederick, rising, and drawing an armchair forward to the fire. "Your walk must have been a long and cheerless one. Let me order some refreshment."

"Not yet," said the Druid, seating himself, and stretching out his hands to the blaze,—hands which were very thin and white, and would have done no discredit to a city dandy. "I have come for a purpose, as you may suppose, and, until that is accomplished, I want nothing."

"I am glad, then, that you braved the storm," said Frederick, drawing his own chair to the fire; "for in two days more I shall have left Glynarth far behind for a time."

"It is that departure, of which I have but just heard, which has brought me here to-night," said the Druid, quietly; "and though you may fancy that I am interfering unnecessarily with your affairs, I hope that you will bear with me for a little while."

"I shall be very glad indeed to have your advice," began Frederick.

"And to disregard it," retorted the other, in the same quiet manner. "You Englishmen are famous for giving good advice to others, and never acting upon it when it is offered to yourselves. The news of this contemplated flight of yours—for it is really nothing else—has filled me with anxiety, not for me and mine, for we are well able to care for ourselves, but for Annie Hughes, in whom I am much interested, and for yourself. If you go away, it is possible, quite possible, that you will never see her again in this world."

"Why should I?" he asked, bitterly; "to see her again would be to deepen the pain which is already tearing my heart now

that I am daily drifting nearer to a marriage
with Miss Montressor. But why should I
never see her again? You surely do not
mean to tell me that personal danger is
hanging over her head?"

"I have every reason to believe that such
is the case," replied the Druid. "You do
not yet seem to be convinced that you have
to deal with a most unscrupulous foe in
the person of Mrs. Montressor. You are
strictly honourable in your dealings with her
daughter, though I confess that to my rustic
mind there is not much honour in marrying
a girl with whom you are sure to be unhappy, and who really cares but very little
for you, and that at the expense of breaking
the heart of a maiden who would be a
priceless treasure to any man. But let that
pass. If your honour forbids you to break
off this engagement, your future mother-in-
law's honour was not sufficiently bright to
restrain her from almost sacrificing Annie
Hughes's life because she was unfortunate
enough to be beloved by you. Even now

she has not forgiven you, and the explanation which you gave to Miss Montressor, an explanation which I vainly sought to put off, has increased her anger. Perhaps, if you remain here, she will not dare to take any open steps against her; and, in any case, your assistance may be needed. You will certainly have an opportunity before long for estimating the integrity of the lady with whose family you are bent upon allying yourself."

"If I thought that my presence would avert or ward off a moment's danger from her I would stay," he said, hesitatingly.

"It will certainly delay the blow," he replied; "it may possibly avert it completely; but whatever course this woman may take in her rage, it will be well for you to remain on the spot. Will you stay?"

"Well, I hardly know," he began, in some perplexity.

"You hardly know whether to believe me or not," was the somewhat bitter interruption; "and yet I have given you strong proofs that I am acting honestly in this matter. What could I gain by libelling this woman, or by offering you marriage with her daughter?" Go your own way if you choose; set me down, as I doubt not you have done, as a charlatan and a pretender, but tell me so clearly and frankly. If you leave Glynarth now, your only remaining chance of escaping from the toils by which you are surrounded is gone for ever."

He spoke earnestly and impressively, and his words carried conviction to Frederick's mind.

"Pardon me for doubting you," he said, rising as he spoke, and offering him his hand; "you have certainly convinced me that you are quite disinterested in this matter. Now, take a calm view of the whole case. What am I to do? Anything rather than marry Miss Montressor."

The stern, harsh features of the young man relaxed slightly as he listened to Frederick's apology.

"We understand each other at last," he said; "and, as to your course, it will be simply this. Visit the house as little as possible; keep a watchful eye, if you can, on Annie Hughes, or, rather, be ready to help her whenever you may be called upon to do so, and leave the rest to me."

"But what are you preparing to do?" asked Frederick.

"What I cannot reveal at present," replied the Druid; "to do so would be to run the risk of defeating myself. This much I may confide in you. Before the arrival of the time appointed for your wedding, Mrs. Montressor will not have an inch of land to call her own; and you will find this to be no empty boast, but a terrible reality—for her. Everything that she prizes, and has sinned for, will be swept away from her possession. Will you trust me so far as to allow me to keep the secret for a little while longer?"

"Most certainly; and, although it seems hardly credible, I have every confidence in you," said his host. "But, allow me to ask, what is your name?"

"I have none," he replied, abruptly, and almost fiercely; "at least, none which could be pronounced by an English tongue. We have done well enough without a name hitherto, and we may as well continue to do so."

"But why are you so hostile to Mrs. Emmerson, or Montressor, or whatever her name may be?" he asked. "Heaven knows I have but small reason to be thankful to her; but I do not feel the same intense enmity towards her as you do."

"I have no particular enmity towards her," he replied, calmly. "I am interested in another and opposing branch of the family; and, so far, I am her enemy; but I have no ill-feeling beyond this. She has sinned deeply, and I am able to punish her."

"I should particularly like to hear the story of your life," said Frederick, advancing towards the bell; "but in the meantime you must take some refreshment. What is

it to be?    Brandy, wine, coffee?—anything
you please.''

"I never drink spirits—indeed, I have
never tasted them in my life," he replied.
"Tea or coffee will be very acceptable."

"And, of course, you will stay here to-
night?"

"Certainly not; we never sleep in
houses," replied the Druid.    "We are
bound by a solemn oath not to do so—
not to depart from our primitive habits.
Indeed, were it not that the women cannot dispense with tea, I might interdict even that."

The tray was brought in, and the servant,
having lingered a moment to pile up the fire
anew, withdrew.

"And now for your story," said his host,
seating himself before the blaze near the
Druid.

"There is nothing very romantic connected with it," he began; "at least, I do
not think so.    Many years ago there resided a young girl, whom I will call Gwen,
with her parents at a small farm near the

village.   She was their only child—the
child, indeed, of their old age; for they had
been married rather later in life than is
usually the case, and this daughter was the
only pledge of their love.   She was beautiful
—not perhaps to the fastidious taste of
Englishmen and those who rank above us,
the common herd; although, as you shall
hear, one of these did not overlook her
charms.   She was pure and innocent—
much too innocent to remain near Montressor House, where the young squire,
the brother of the late owner, was then
squandering his money and trying to ruin
a fine constitution.   He saw her one day
and was smitten by her charms.   Would to
God that she had died before that day!"

His voice shook with emotion, but, re-
covering himself, he went on :—

"You may imagine the result.   Flattered
by the preference of the greatest man who
had ever crossed her narrow path, she met
him in secret, and his reluctance to disclose
their love affair to her parents gave her no

uneasiness. Her sin was a light one when we remember her ignorance and his wiles; but it was heavily visited upon her. She trusted him, and she fell. It was the old story of trusting innocence and designing craft, as old as Eve and the serpent, which your books speak about.

"Matters came to a crisis at last, for a son was born, and her father, maddened by the dishonour of his daughter, appealed in vain to her betrayer. You English may scoff at the Welsh peasant's proneness to this sin, but there is a purer love for virtue in his breast than amongst his Saxon brethren. The squire treated his remonstrances with indifference at first, and then with open contempt. Why should he heed the destruction of the poor man's rosebud when that poor man happened to be one of his own tenants? And so he had to bear his sorrowful burden; and Gwen, almost broken-hearted by her lover's desertion, pined away day after day.

"She met him one evening, and re-

proached him with his treachery. No one
knew exactly what took place in that interview, but it is certain that he treated her
with the same contempt which he had exhibited towards her father. An hour afterwards a labourer, returning home from the
fields, saw a woman's form hurrying towards
the sea; and, curious as to what her object
might be, he followed her, but could not
overtake her. He watched her as she made
her way to the brow of a cliff overhanging
the dark rolling waters of the bay; and then,
for the first time, a suspicion as to her intention crossed his sluggish mind. It was too
late to save her. The sound of approaching
footsteps caused her to turn her face towards
him—a white, agonized face, which haunted
him for years afterwards—and then, clasping
her uplifted hands to heaven, with one last
despairing cry for mercy, she sprang into
the depths below.

"There was rest there, perhaps, for the
poor child of sorrow, crushed beneath the
dull weight of misery. The waves en-

gulphed her in their cold embrace, and the
horror-stricken man returned to tell his tale
to the grief-laden parents.

"She was my mother; and can you
wonder, therefore, that I do not love the
Montressor race? The man who was my
father found an unhonoured grave in a
foreign land; but his sins have been even
eclipsed by his successors who now hold his
broad acres. But the day of retribution is
at hand. Men may prate as they will of a
vengeance which comes not in this world;
but mine will fall upon this accursed house
in the apparent fulness of its power. And
now, will you stay?"

"I will," said Frederick, moved by the
recital of his sorrows. "A strange destiny
has brought me into the midst of this
tragedy in real life, and I will remain to the
end, whatever it may be."

"It will be a bright ending for you,"
said the Druid, mournfully; "but for me—
but I dare not look forward. Good-night,
and remember."

Placing his hat upon his head and again concealing his features, he went away, leaving Frederick wrapped in deep and anxious thought.

# CHAPTER VII.

### A DRUID SETTLEMENT.

FREDERICK had decided upon staying in
Glynarth whatever might be the issue of the
strange entanglement in which he found
himself, but beyond an occasional call upon
Miss Montressor he did not often leave the
Lodge.    On these occasions Mrs. Montressor discreetly allowed the "young people," as she always called them, to converse
with one another alone, but when Frederick
was leaving she always made a point of
chiding him for his very evident neglect of
his future bride, though, of course, she
knew perfectly well the state of things.
Mr. Emmerson came up one afternoon, a
most unusual proceeding for him, for there

was not much love lost between the two men, and they never met without a sense of restraint.

"I thought I would call upon you," he said, after the usual platitudes about the weather, "to ask what arrangements are to be made about the wedding. It is really time that something was done."

It seemed to be a settled matter in his mind that the ceremony was to take place, the details only required consideration.

"I hardly know, for I confess that I have not considered the matter," said Frederick, who was somewhat disposed to speak out plainly, and declare his wish to break off the engagement, "there is no particular hurry that I know of."

"The time agreed upon will expire in a month, and the affair may as well be settled then, if you have no objection," replied Emmerson, fixing his cunning eyes on Frederick's face as he spoke, and his gaze made the young man uncomfortable, and even alarmed, for apart from the question

of honour, he was almost afraid of this man
and his wife.  Of physical courage he was
not deficient, but the evils which he dreaded
were shadowy and intangible, and, therefore, were difficult to combat with.  For
Annie's sake, too, as well as his own, he
feared the consequences of an open rupture
with a desperate man and an equally desperate woman, for such he had every reason
to believe them to be.

"We will say in six weeks, then," he
said, in full reliance upon the Druid's
power to bring matters to a crisis before
then.  "Six weeks from to-day, if you
like."

Emmerson objected at first to this further
delay, but eventually agreed to it, and the
day of the month was definitely fixed, subject, as Frederick remarked, to the approval
of the ladies.  Then they strutted out into
the stables and around the grounds, and
afterwards Emmerson returned to Montressor House to report progress.  Frederick
had promised to call on the next day to

discuss various matters connected with the wedding, and at last Mrs. Emmerson flattered herself that the affair was in full train.

Wearied and disgusted, he took his hat and set out on foot to the place where the Druids made their head-quarters. It was never very difficult to find, for it was known to most of the people in the surrounding neighbourhood, though but few of them knew anything of the tortuous intricacies of the place. That knowledge the initiated few kept to themselves, and it had been useful on more than one occasion.

He could not present himself at the entrance to the cave, for he was ignorant of the manner by which admission could be gained, and he felt certain that he would not have to wait long before his friend made his appearance.

He therefore seated himself upon a rock, and lighting a cigar, began to smoke. It was nearly dark, and the burning end glowed in the gloom as he inhaled the fragrant fumes, but the Druid did not come.

He had been there perhaps for half-an-hour when his well-known voice was heard at his side.

"Meditating in the darkness," he said, "darkness within and without—dark and gloomy everywhere."

"Yes, and perhaps we are happier thus than if we had more light," said Frederick, flinging away the weed; "we ought not to murmur at our lot, for it might be infinitely worse than it is."

"And it might be infinitely better," replied the Druid; "yours is cheerless enough, for instance, if you had no prospect whatever of a bright to-morrow."

"That reminds me of the errand which brought me here to-night," said Frederick; "Mr. Emmerson visited me this afternoon, and we fixed the date for the wedding, the 26th of next month."

"That was rather an extreme step," observed the Druid, gravely, "could you not have avoided it?"

"Only by refusing absolutely to fulfil my

promise, and that I will not do, for the truth is, I am rather afraid of that man."

"You ought to fear his wife a good deal more, but perhaps it is well to avoid driving them to desperation now," said the other. "Six weeks—that will be amply sufficient. A week might possibly be sufficient, a fortnight at most, and then Mrs. Emmerson, as she calls herself, will hear something of me."

"Has she never heard of you yet?"

"I cannot say—I am well known to the people here, and she may have heard of the chief Druid," he said, drawing himself up a little proudly, "but she does not dream that I am interested in her movements, nor that I have the power and will to thwart her schemes."

"Then my purpose in coming here is accomplished," said Frederick; "it is extremely distasteful to me to have to listen to plans and projects for a marriage which I sincerely hope will never take place, but of course if your plan, whatever it may be, fails, I will fulfil my pledge."

"We never fail in our undertakings," replied the Druid, with a strange smile, "and in this case there are no difficulties in the way. I could drive mother and daughter away from Glynarth to-night if I chose, but I do not choose. My plans are not yet ripe for execution, and we must wait a little longer. And now, I have been barely hospitable to you in your visits here. Would it give you any satisfaction to see some of the mysteries of this place?"

"It would delight me above everything," said Frederick; "I have long wished to see your mode of life, but fancying that you would not care to reveal your secrets, I never dared to ask you."

"We have but little to conceal," said the Druid, as he led the way to the cave; "we have wonders here, but to us there is nothing wonderful in them, and to a truly inquiring mind the sages of our race have ever been willing to manifest their power. Follow me."

He passed down the dark entrance until

they stood before the door, which was
opened by one of the old women whom he
had seen on a previous occasion. She
greeted the Druid with a low reverence,
which he acknowledged with a smile, and
then led the way to the farther end of the
room. Here he drew aside a curtain, and
disclosed another passage, rather narrower
and darker than the first, and along this
they passed. Sounds of music and revelry
reached them as they drew near the end,
and after tapping at another door which
barred the way, it was thrown open, and a
moving sight presented itself.

It was a large apartment, or rather a hall,
which had been formed out of a natural
cave. The roof was shaped like a dome,
and far up was a small aperture, which in
the daytime admitted light, and there were
many small openings to permit of the passage of the air. The walls were formed of
solid rock, and in rude niches about a
hundred torches blazed, filling the place
with a flood of light. But the inmates of

this subterranean cave attracted Frederick's attention more than the wonders of the structure. A very large number of young people of both sexes were dancing briskly when the Druid and his friend entered, whilst a blind harper at one end discoursed music which would have been scouted in the ball-rooms of fashion, but which had a melody and a charm all its own to the young hearts within its influence. There was nothing extraordinary in their attire; it was simply the dress usually worn by the young men and girls whom he met every day.

Evidently the fun had been fast and furious, but the entrance of the stranger brought it to an abrupt termination. The strains of the harp ceased, and the dancers gazed with ill-concealed suspicion upon Frederick, who was known to many of them, but the Druid restored their peace of mind. Waving his hand, he said, " Ewch ymlaen ; mae heddwch yn y gwersyll." *

* Go on ; there is peace in the camp.

He led Frederick to a seat near one side of the hall, and sat down near him.

"Explain this scene," said the Englishman, curiously; "I confess that I do not understand it."

"That is easily done," replied the other. "You were no doubt under the impression that our life is a gloomy and ascetic one, and that we forbid scenes of this kind; on the contrary, we encourage them. There never were grander balls than those on the green-sward in the days before Cæsar landed his legions on our shores, when our Cymric forefathers returned from the battle-field, or celebrated a marriage, or some other event of a joyous nature. To-night we celebrate a day which to your ideas might seem to be a mournful one. Four seasons have gone by since a father of our race passed to his honoured rest, and we are celebrating the anniversary."

"Dancing to commemorate a man's death!" cried Frederick, half incredulously.

"Yes; why not?" he asked quickly.

"Your teachers tell you, as heathen philosophers have done before them, that death
is a wonderful gain ; and that it would be
worth a man's while to endure the pains of
dissolution many times over for the sake of
witnessing the glories of the spirit land,
and yet you weep and lament when a dear
one is taken away. It is because that dear
one is lost to your sight for ever, and you
are unable to grasp the shadow of consola-
tion held out to you ; but with us the case
is different. We grieve as you do for his
bodily absence, but we can speak to him,
we can commune with his soul whenever
we desire it. He is released from the ills
of life, and has reached the home of light,
and for his sake we rejoice—and for our
own, too, for he is ever filling our minds
with new light. Every sage who has gone
to his rest hovers around us, and opens new
founts of knowledge."

"Then, in time, you must learn all that
is to be known in the world," observed
Frederick.

"If our minds were capable of receiving
this knowledge, we might undoubtedly
penetrate all the secrets of nature," replied
the Druid; "but we are so fettered by our
littleness and insignificance that we cannot
thoroughly comprehend even the simplest
and earliest truths. But let that pass. You
understand now how when others weep
we rejoice; when the outside world is
sorrowful we are glad."

"And who are all these young people?"

"You must have seen some of them
before. Do you not recognise that youth
who is staring so earnestly upon us from
yonder corner?"

Frederick's eye was bent in the direction
indicated, and saw his own stable-boy,
a lad whom he had engaged from the
village.

"I see that you have met him before,"
observed the Druid, with a quiet smile.
"He is a villager, and so are most of those
before you. All of them reside near, and
all of them are nominally members of our

community, though many of them, I fear, regard our faith as a national rather than a religious institution. We have only a few old men and women who reside here beside myself; the rest come only on special occasions."

" But many of these young people attend places of Christian worship," remarked Frederick.

" True; many of them, as I said, come here because their fathers did so before them, just as men go to church or chapel because they have been accustomed to do so," was the Druid's reply; " but we still receive them, for in the end we must conquer. We have withstood ages of persecution and discouragement, and the very fact that we exist at all is, to my mind, a proof that Druidism is not destined to die. In the meantime, until brighter days dawn, we are content to wait, and to retain our hold upon the people as well as we can. But listen ! "

The dancing had ceased, and all were

listening to the old harper, who was accompanying his harp with a rather weak and quavering voice; but not a whisper was heard as he sang. The words in English would be somewhat thus :—

### PRINCE DAVID'S FAREWELL.

The last prince of Cambria lay musing in sorrow
   The eve of that day which was fraught with his doom,
Awaiting the dawn of that voiceless to-morrow
   When Death would encircle his soul with its gloom.
" Fair mountains of Cambria, proud strongholds of free-
    dom,
   No more on their summits my footsteps shall roam ;
In death I still love thee, in bitterest thraldom,
   My heart clings to Cymru, my childhood's sweet home.

" The last of my race, I depart to my fathers,
   The strains of the *telyn*\* no more shall I hear ;
And round my own land a dark tempest still gathers—
   The groans of its heroes still ring in my ear.
My spirit shall wing its far flight from its prison,
   But still e'en in death I will murmur thy name ;
No Briton in death to his land can be faithless,
   I die for thy glory, thy honour, thy fame ! "

A murmur of approbation ran through the assembly, and a jug of hot ale was

* Harp.

handed to the harper to refresh his jaded
powers, and the dance began anew.

"We will leave them to their enjoyment,"
said the chief Druid, rising; "there is
one scene more which I wish to show you.
Come!"

He led the way back again to the outer
apartment, and then down another passage,
but this one was lighted by torches placed
at intervals in the wall. They descended a
few steps cut out from the earth, and passed
through another door. Then a strange view
presented itself.

The place in which they stood was a
much smaller apartment than either of those
which they had left, but it was decorated
with quaint, fantastic paintings, evidently
executed by some untutored hand. A leek
elaborately wrought in gold was fixed at one
end, and beneath it was a small rude altar
with no pretensions whatever to decoration
or splendour. A smouldering fire was burning upon it, and Frederick noticed that his
companion paused some dozen paces from it.

"This is the place where the remnant of our faith assemble to adore the Deity," he said in a low, reverent voice; "and you are the only stranger who has been admitted here, at least since my earliest recollections. It is simple and unpretending, as you see; and yet there is as much of what you call piety assembled here in our hours of devotion as in the most splendid shrines of Christian worship."

"Why is that fire kept burning upon the altar?" asked Frederick.

"That fire has been burning for ages and centuries, and has never been extinguished since the day when it was first kindled by the Deity himself. You may smile at the superstition if you will; but it has certainly been burning here in this very spot from the first day when this temple was opened, and that was many hundreds of years ago."

"I do not dispute that, nor do I mock at your faith," said Frederick; "it is, in any case, a very venerable one, but I confess I do not understand it."

"And you probably never will," was the frank reply; "but we who have been taught to adhere to it since childhood, and who have been nurtured in the midst of its glorious traditions, we alone can appreciate its genius."

"But this very fact will effectually prevent it from spreading again, and gaining new adherents."

"Possibly; but then, if everybody were wise, wisdom would be no pleasure. Let us leave here."

They returned again to what we may call the ball-room, and there the evening's entertainments were in full progress.

"Would you like to hear one more song before you go?" asked the Druid, as they entered.

"If you please," replied Frederick; and stepping up to the minstrel, the Druid spoke a few words to him.

Again the dancing ceased, and the old man sang :—

" I dwell in a valley, removed from the pleasures
　　Which charm and delight the proud hearts of the gay ;
　My wealth is but little, and simple my treasures,
　　And yet I am happier day after day.
　The murmuring brooklet is music more glorious
　　Than anthems which spring from the fountain of art;
　I crave not the rank of the great and the famous ;
　　My sleep is unbroken, and light is my heart.


" When daylight departeth I trudge from the meadows,
　　And watch with my children the sun as it wanes ;
　I love thus to gaze on its fast-deepening shadows,
　　When darkness enfolds rocks, hills, mountains, and
　　　　plains.
　My bliss is undimmed by a trace of dark sorrow,
　　My end will be peaceful, my rest shall be sweet ;
　No dread in the future, no care for to-morrow—
　　The happiest man that on earth you will meet."


"Such is our life," said the Druid, as they stood together once more in the open air; "and I have shown it to you in order to dispel any false ideas you may have formed respecting it. And now, good-night. I have a journey before me to-morrow; but on the third night from this, at the same hour, be here again. I may have something to show you."

They parted after a warm farewell; and deeply interested by the strange sights he had witnessed, Frederick wended his way homewards.

" One faith the more in this world can make but little difference," he mused; " but I doubt if my nameless friend, with all his earnestness, really knows what he is believing in. But then he is no worse off than thousands of others who profess to teach and enlighten the world."

And with this consoling reflection he dismissed the subject, and his mind reverted to the old and absorbing question—that of his impending marriage with Maria Mon tressor.

# CHAPTER VIII.

## MR. EMMERSON'S TROUBLES.

FREDERICK called on the following morning at Montressor House, and found Maria and her mother in the morning room. Mrs. Emmerson was rather more sharp and disagreeable than usual, though she made an effort to be kind and affable; but it was evident that she was not altogether pleased with his conduct.

"Your visits are really refreshing, Mr. Danvers," she said; "they come so seldom, and you always make them so brief."

"I am sorry if I have given you any cause for complaint," he said, coldly, disregarding an appealing look from Maria; 'but I thought you understood the state of

affairs sufficiently well to know that I do
not care to come too often to a place where
my reception is never very cordial."

"Explain yourself, if you please," said
the lady, with freezing politeness. "Maria,
this *gentleman* and myself must have a little
conversation, and you had better withdraw."

The girl saw the impending blow, and
dreaded the result. The bond by which
she held Frederick was already so slender
that it might very easily be snapped, and
she was therefore anxious to soothe her
irritated and impolitic mother.

"Do not be angry, mamma," she said,
with a meaning glance; "Frederick meant
nothing, and I am sure did not wish to hurt
your feelings."

"Leave the room, child," exclaimed the
angry woman; "he can tell me for himself
what he meant."

She almost pushed her out of the apartment, and then returned to the charge.

"Now, sir, you have been hanging about
my daughter for a long time, and have

treated her in a way which no woman can
tolerate. I want an explanation of all
this."

Frederick was standing near the open
window, with his hat in his hand, listening
with a perfectly calm and unmoved face.
As the subject had been in a measure forced
upon him, he was determined to break off
the engagement for ever.

"I should like to know exactly what I
have to explain," he said, quietly.

"What you have to explain? Why,
everything, sir," she said, furiously, for
she had quite lost the command of her
temper; "you proposed to my daughter."

"Pardon me, but I think you are wrong,"
he interrupted.

"You are generous to remind me of that
circumstance," she said, with a bitter sneer;
"you paid attention to the poor girl until,
carried away by her feelings, she gave you
a hint as to the state of her affections,
and you made no objection. You were
formally engaged, you cannot deny that;

and, notwithstanding this, you have neglected her in every possible manner. I
can guess the reason, for every one in the
village knows how low your taste is in this
respect."

"We will not discuss the question of
low taste," he said, gravely and significantly; "but if your remark was intended
as an insult to Miss Hughes, I cannot
listen to it. I would willingly have avoided
this discussion if I could; but now that you
have introduced it, I must beg of you to
listen to me."

"Go on, sir," she said, folding her arms,
as if to listen, while the same bitter sneer
played upon her lips.

"The engagement between Miss Montressor and myself was not of my seeking,"
he continued; "I believed that her feelings
were to a certain extent involved, and at
that time I was also under the impression
that Miss Hughes was lost to me for ever.
I therefore assented to the arrangement
which she proposed; but since then the

barrier between Miss Hughes and myself
has been broken down. You will observe
that I am perfectly frank and candid with
you."

"Very frank, indeed," she said, mockingly; "and then you are anxious to try
your fortune again with a girl who has
discarded you once."

"She discarded me, as you call it, at
your instigation, I believe, and was compelled to do so by what I have reason to
believe was a perfectly false threat," he
said; and this arrow shot home, for she
changed colour and was visibly embarrassed.

"I advised her for her own good," she
said, defiantly. "If she has represented
our conversation to you in a false light,
I cannot help it."

"Miss Hughes has said but very little
to me about your unwarrantable interference
at all," he replied; "but from other sources
I think I fully understand the part you
played."

"And this, of course, was the reason

you wished to shirk an engagement which every man of honour would regard as sacred?"

"I have not tried to escape from it—except, indeed, that I had a conversation with Miss Montressor, in which I explained to her that I had never loved her as she ought to be loved or as I believe she deserves to be loved, and that it would be far better for both of us to terminate an engagement which could only result in unhappiness to one, possibly to both of us. She refused to release me, and until to-day it was my intention, if she still persisted in holding me to my promise, to fulfil it."

"And you have changed your mind to-day then?" she asked, in an anxious voice; for the violence of her passion had passed away, and she was already beginning to regret her extreme hastiness.

"Most certainly," he replied; "after this scene I must positively put an end to it. It has gone too far already, and I deeply regret ever having entered upon it.   I shall always regard Miss Montressor with feelings of friendship, but nothing more."

"And this is your final decision?" she exclaimed, with renewed anger.

"It is.   I am sorry that I have unwittingly been the cause of wounding her feelings, but we can never be anything more to each other than friends."

"My daughter, sir, will no doubt be highly flattered by your friendship," she said, mockingly; "especially when she recalls your very honourable and gentlemanly conduct."

"I am quite satisfied with my own conduct," he said, coldly; "and as for honour, there does not appear to be very much of it amongst the aristocracy of Glynarth."

She flushed angrily at this covert taunt, and again her vexation found vent.

"You will regret this step to the last moment of your life," she said, rising and drawing herself erect; "this will be the worst day's work you ever did in your life."

"If you threaten me I must wish you good-morning," he said, turning to depart; "we have conversed quite long enough on the subject."

Without deigning to make any reply she rang the bell, and a footman appeared.

"Show this *gentleman* to the door," she said, with marked emphasis, "and never admit him here again."

He bowed gravely as he left the room, heeding not this public insult, and he was so delighted to stand in the open air free once more that he gave the grinning servant a sovereign.

"Missis is in a temper this morning, sir," said the man; "she very often is."

"My good fellow, I am not at all sorry, and it is not probable that you will ever see me here again."

The footman was sorry to hear this, for but few of his mistress's visitors had treated him so well.

And thus Frederick went away from Montressor House, fully intending never to set foot within its portals again, but he was destined to do so ere long, and that under strange and exciting circumstances.

He walked homeward with a lighter heart than he had experienced for many a long day. He was at liberty once more to woo and win the sweet girl who had gained his love—to fall again at her feet, and to whisper words of affection.

" What an escape I have had," he mused. " She would have been a terrible mother-in-law."

And she of whom he was thinking was standing at the window, with her daughter, watching his retreating form.

" Take your last fond look at your cava-lier," she said, sneeringly.   " He has thrown you aside completely."

" Oh, mamma, you have broken my heart," her daughter wailed, as she sank upon a couch; "you do not dream how I loved him."

" Loved him ! " echoed her astonished parent; " what absurd nonsense !  It would

be better if you were in love with our stable-
boy than with 'him, precious idiot as he is."

"What can we do, mamma?" asked the
girl. "Is there no way of bringing him
back?"

"None whatever," she answered, gloomily.
"Your engagement is at an end, and we
have nothing now to do but to be revenged."

"No, no; let it end here, then," pleaded
Maria. "Do not injure him, as you love me."

"I may not injure him," she answered;
"but this wretched upstart who has en-
tangled him must be punished, and that
heavily.  Send Mr. Emmerson to me."

She went out and directed one of the
servants to call his master.  That gentleman, however, had not yet left his dressing-
room, but sent to say that he would be
down presently.

He came, and sauntered into the room in
his old indifferent manner.  Care and trouble were lowering ominously above his head,
and he knew it; but he still preserved his
careless, haughty demeanour.

"What is the matter?" he asked, as he noticed his lady's agitated manner. "Have any of the servants broken the china or absconded?"

"Some one else has absconded, Mr. Emmerson," she said, harshly. "I have just had a visit from Mr. Danvers, and what do you think he has told me?"

"I have not the remotest idea," he said, though he could form a tolerably accurate idea.

"He refused finally and decisively to fulfil his engagement with Maria."

"I rather expected it," he said, carelessly.

"You did? and yet you never mentioned your suspicions to me!" she exclaimed.

"You could see as well as I could the state of the case," he said; "he never wished to marry her at all."

"In any case he shall suffer for it," she said, angrily; "he must be taught that he cannot trifle with *me* thus."

"You have plenty of work on your hands

without undertaking any more," he said, roughly. "What are we to do with Edmund Montressor's last letter?"

This mysterious individual had just sent a fresh demand for money, and intimated that unless it was met more promptly than the last request he had made, he might think it advisable to take the estate into his own hands.

"I am at a loss to understand what his real intentions are," she replied; "the more I consider his conduct the more extraordinary it appears to me. I thought it strange at the time that after we had made an attempt upon his life he should go away quietly, and how he went away I cannot imagine, if your story be true, and thus leave me in undisturbed possession."

"He seems to be a strange fellow in everything," he remarked.

"Yes; but I am not disposed to remain any longer in this state of suspense," she continued; "I will go to London and see him for myself. If I cannot make some arrangement with him, something else may suggest itself," she added, significantly.

"Very good, my dear, I leave it entirely in your hands," he said, and then he left the room in search of some breakfast.

"She is a wonderful woman," he mused, the second man who that morning had been meditating on Mrs. Emmerson's virtues, "a very wonderful woman, but she will get me into a most ungodly scrape, and I don't at all see the end of this business. I wish I did."

The post arrived in another hour, and there was a letter for him, addressed in the same rude handwriting which had previously caused Mrs. Emmerson some uneasiness. If an opportunity had been afforded her she might have instituted an inquiry into its contents, but the owner of the mysterious missive made his appearance before she had leisure to do so.

"A letter for you, Henry," she said, handing it to him, "you seem to have a rather uneducated correspondent."

"Education spoils a man and a woman too, my dear," he said, sententiously, as he deposited it in his pocket ; " I like nature in its wild untutored state."

" Don't talk nonsense," she said, angrily, " if you do not wish to tell me who the writer is, at least spare me your sermons."

"Very good, my dear, and, therefore, I will go for a stroll whilst you master your budget of news."

He strolled out into the grounds to a sequestered nook, where he was not likely to be observed, and then, after lighting a short clay pipe, which was a special favourite of his, he drew forth his wife's letter, and examined the address. It was, in truth, a nearly illegible scrawl, and the stamp had been affixed at one of the bottom corners.

" It is not much to look at, certainly," he mused ; "but she never was much of a literary character. How very inconvenient it is to have two wives, especially when you don't care very much for either of them.

And this letter, after all I have said and written to her about annoying me!  I may as well see what is in it.  Nothing very affectionate, I'll wager."

He opened it and read the contents with a lowering countenance.

"My Dear Husband," it began, but the spelling was far from perfect, "I am quite tired of waiting for your return, and sick of promises which you never keep, so I mean to come to the place where you are staying at to find out just what you are doing.  You must intend to leave me altogether, or else you would have come back before now, and I shan't let you do that.  So I hope to see you soon, and I am sure you will be glad to see me."

"She will ruin me," he groaned, as he crushed the letter in his hand; "just when I am beginning to be comfortably settled in life, and to feel myself on firm ground at last, one wife threatens to go up to London,

the last place in the world where I would wish
her to go, and the other is coming down upon
me, and will, of course, denounce me.   She
never shall, by heaven !   I swear she shall
never pull down the structure I have been
so long in erecting."

For a few minutes he was lost in deep
and anxious thought, trying to devise some
method of averting the dreaded visit without
further involving himself in crime, but he
could think of nothing likely to meet the
case.

"It is my fate," he muttered, "every
step which I take seems to lead me deeper
into guilt, and yet I cannot help myself.
She must be removed at any cost, and then
I can easily settle Mrs. Montressor—I beg
her pardon, Mrs. Emmerson."

The lady had gone into the village on a
visit to the schools, and here she met Mr.
Campbell, whom she had not seen for some
time.

"It seems as if all my friends are desert-
ing me, Mr. Campbell," she said, with a

sigh; "you have not been near the house for a very long time."

"I mean to come soon," he said, for since her marriage he had held aloof, not being able to appreciate Mr. Emmerson's merits, and suspecting that the marriage was not wholly based upon love. "I am collecting subscriptions for the repairing of the church, and I hope you will assist us."

"Come and put my liberality to the test," she said, anxious to please him so far as possible; "I shall be very pleased to see you."

And she sailed out from the schoolroom, followed by the admiring gaze of some fifty pairs of eyes belonging to the young village hopefuls.

As she walked homewards an old woman passed by who stared her fully in the face— an old woman whom she feared with an un- defined and yet powerful dread. It was Sian. She had evidently been making some purchases in the village, for an old basket, with a leather strap as a handle, was on her arm, filled with groceries and other things.

Mrs. Emmerson returned her glance with a scornful and defiant look, but she fancied that pity was blended largely with the old woman's hatred. Why should she pity her? she asked herself. Had she not fallen to a depth of degradation, indeed, when this old crone could pity *her*? And yet, as she walked slowly homewards, the fear of some impending misfortune haunted her, and filled her mind with uneasiness. The beginning of the end was nigh at hand.

## CHAPTER IX.

### THE DEAD MEN'S COUNCIL.

WHEN Mrs. Emmerson was thus in a state
of mingled alarm and anger, the man who
had escaped from her toils was much more
pleasantly occupied. Early that afternoon
Frederick hastened to the Glyn, to an-
nounce his release to Annie, and, impatient to hold her once more in his arms,
to whisper again the old sweet story, the
way seemed unusually long.

He had not walked that way since the
evening when he found her in the churchyard, and everything looked brighter and
more lovely, tinted with the rose-light
which filled his own mind. It was not a
very romantic walk either, for fat pigs lay

grunting lazily in the road—for the county
was famous for pigs and parsons—and he
could see hot and thirsty men ploughing in
the fields here and there. How he pitied
them, as he compared their life with his
own, and yet, a few days before, he might
have envied them their freedom from the
troubles which beset him! The magician's
wand had dispelled his difficulties, and he
could hardly realize his own happiness.

He came to the house, and stood for a
moment gazing in silence upon it. The
gate was closed, and the blinds were drawn
over all the windows, to exclude the heat
and fierce light of the sun. The garden
and the grass-plots presented a hot and
dusty appearance, and not a sign of life
could be seen anywhere. The whole place
had a sleepy, lifeless look, and even the
hens seemed to have gone to roost. As
for the old women, they always took a nap
in the afternoon, and at other times, when
they had nothing more pleasant to do.

He pushed open the garden-gate, and

knocked at the door, which was opened by
a servant-girl whom Annie had engaged.
As a rule, her mistress attended to the front
door herself, but this afternoon she was
occupied with some domestic duties in the
kitchen, and had therefore sent the servant.

"Is Miss Hughes at home?" he asked.

"Yes, sir," replied the girl, who, without
waiting to invite him in, vanished to summon her mistress.

Left to himself, Frederick walked into the
dear old familiar sitting-room, and waited.
He stood looking out of the window, and
wondered why Annie did not come; but the
poor girl was so overcome by his arrival,
that she was compelled to pause for a time
to recover herself.

She entered the room at last, and, in
another moment, was locked in his arms.

"My darling!" he whispered, "it has
come at last. We will forget the miserable, unhappy past, and live only for one
another."

Then she knew that he was free once

more—free, indeed, from Miss Montressor, but a hopeless captive, nevertheless, and a captive who hugged his own chains.

Ah! there was an amount of kissing and hugging, and whispering, which would have shocked the old women in the cottages without, if they could have seen it, but which was intensely pleasant to those concerned in it. It is vain to attempt to repeat the incoherent love-speeches, and the soft words, which were uttered during that first hour. The man must be a miserable wretch, indeed, who has not some scene like this to look back upon; some sacred recess in his heart, where the sweet echoes of a woman's voice still lingers, though perhaps years may have elapsed since he heard its accents. And as the darkening shadows of life cluster thickly around that one sacred spot, its brightness shines forth with increasing lustre.

They settled down, at last, for some sober conversation, and now we may return to them. Annie had been extremely ill since that memorable visit to her brother's grave, and her face was yet pale and wan.

"You must have been very ill, my darling," he said, tenderly, "and I never heard of it."

"No, I took care that it should not be known in the village, lest you should hear of it," she answered, with a faint smile; "I thought that you had sufficient cause for trouble as it was; but that is over now. Tell me all about your interview with Mrs. Emmerson."

Of course she was not devoid of curiosity —she would not have been a true woman if it were otherwise—but she was grieved for Maria's sake. In the wealth of happiness which had come upon her, she could afford to be compassionate to her less fortunate rival.

"Poor girl, I am very sorry for her," she said, with a sigh; "she will feel it very deeply."

"And so am I, but it is better that the sorrow should come now than in after-years, when it cannot be lightened nor removed," he said, "when a step would have been taken which would certainly consign us both to lifelong misery. We will forget it, dearest. It is too painful a subject to be dwelt upon."

And if they did not forget it, at least they did not revert to it again.

That evening was the beginning of a new life to Frederick Danvers. Never had he been so completely happy. Sitting opposite to Annie in the arm-chair, he smoked a great number of cigars, for which she took him to task, but still confessed that she liked the fragrant odour, and built up many a bright castle in the air, some of which were, indeed, afterwards realized. And then, as the evening advanced, she made tea, and he insisted upon the production of some of her famous jam of home manu-facture, which he declared to be much superior to any that ever came from the hands of Messrs. Crosse and Blackwell. He never spent such a delightful evening.

I can see one of my readers smile, as he comes to the conclusion that Frederick Danvers was an ass; that a dinner at the Star and Garter (of famous memory), or a supper at Evans's, and a box at Covent Garden, with perhaps a bottle of champagne afterwards, at one of those seductive temples of Bacchus in the Haymarket, where the hospitalities of the place are dispensed by half-a-dozen smiling Hebes, who have a weakness for "fizz" and coffee and brandy, would be infinitely better than bread and butter and jam in a farmhouse with a Welsh rustic, as he would probably call her, however pretty and lovable she might be. You may be right, my friend, but tastes differ. The ballet is apt to be slow sometimes, and fairy queens are becoming rather too numerous and commonplace. And a sleepy farmhouse in a remote corner in Wales is sometimes very pleasant, after a long course of Haymarket festivities at one o'clock in the morning.

He went away, after staying long beyond

the usual time, and not before Annie had
lectured him severely for staying so long.
It was a warm and rather sultry evening,
and, as the road was uphill, he did not walk
very rapidly; so that it was between nine
and ten before he found himself again in the
avenue of the Lodge.

Here he met Mr. Campbell, who was coming from the house.

"This is the second time this evening
that I have called," said the vicar, as they
shook hands; "not that I have any particular business, but I thought you might
have something to tell me, and I have not
seen you for a very long time. I have
noticed that you never come to church
now."

"I am very sorry, my dear sir," said
Frederick, laughingly; "but do not chide
me to-night. I am too happy to wish for
a reproof, however mild it might be. I am
delighted to see you, and I fancy that you
have heard of my dismissal from Montressor
House."

They were walking arm-in-arm together
up to the house.

"There is no one within five miles of the
village who has not heard of it," said Mr.
Campbell, with a smile, "but I must say that
you bear the shock with wonderful composure."

"Yes, but I find it hard to convince myself that it is quite real," said Frederick,
more seriously.  "This morning I had not
the least expectation of terminating this
engagement, which, you have no doubt
guessed, had become painful to me.  What
version is afloat of the affair?"

"Oh! it is said that you offended Mrs.
Emmerson in some way, and that she
ordered you away from the house," said the
vicar; "but I am quite curious to know the
real state of affairs.  I never understood
your conduct towards the lady from the first,
and unless it is trespassing too far upon
you, I should be very pleased to hear the
facts of the case."

They were seated now in Frederick's
study, and he ordered refreshments.

"It is right that you should be made acquainted with the real facts," said Frederick; "from first to last the matter stood thus:" and he narrated the history of the engagement, touching very lightly upon Maria's part in it, and giving a complete outline of Mrs. Emmerson's taunts and accusations that morning.

"I saw her this afternoon," said the vicar, when he had told him all, "and she took me to task for not calling; but the fact is, there are strange rumours afloat concerning her, emanating no one knows exactly where; and her conduct to Miss Hughes was simply infamous. By the way, I presume you were making your peace with her this evening?"

"Yes, I am proud and glad to say that she will be my wife in as short a time as possible."

"I congratulate you most sincerely," said the clergyman, cordially; "if any one could have induced me to renounce bachelor-hood, it would have been Miss Hughes, but

as she never cared to do so, I must stand by
to see her carried off by a bolder and more
fortunate man."

He spoke in a tone of pleasant banter,
but if Frederick could have read the secrets
of his heart he would have found a little
romance lurking there, a love which was
never suspected by the outside world, and
of which even the object of this secret
affection was ignorant.   There had been
moments in the young clergyman's life
when the tenderest feelings of man's heart
had been awakened in his breast, but he
himself could almost rejoice that this
temptation had been removed from his path.

"I held aloof partly because of these
rumours," he continued, "and partly because I am doubtful as to her husband's
antecedents.  On the one or two occasions when I have met him he has hardly
treated me with the respect due to my office,
and as Mrs. Emmerson always persists in
discussing the idle gossip of the day whenever I go there, I have not felt inclined to

go too frequently. She promised me a subscription towards the church this afternoon, however, and so far I ought to be grateful. I trust that you will help us too."

Frederick could not repress a smile at this adroit way of introducing the restoration of the church.

"I shall be very happy to contribute," he said, "and if it were not that the church where Annie usually attends is available, I would ask you to spare the old place until after our marriage."

"Miss Hughes will prefer her own church, I fancy," said Mr. Campbell; "the church in which she has done so much good. In fact, she has been worth half-a-dozen curates to me."

"Then I hope that she will still take an interest in every good cause," said Frederick, kindly; "but allow me to give you a gentle hint. If Mrs. Emmerson has promised you a subscription I should advise you to call upon her for it as quickly as you can."

" You surely do not mean to suggest that
these rumours about Edmund Montressor
and his supposed existence are true ? "

" I have never heard of Edmund Montressor, and therefore am quite ignorant as
to the precise danger which is impending
over Mrs. Emmerson, but that there is some
great and imminent danger I am quite convinced."

" Then I shall certainly call to-morrow,"
said the clergyman, anxious to secure the
subscription ; "and as I must be at work
early in the morning, I will wish you good-
night."

It will be observed that he never referred
to the Druid nor to his acquaintance with
him.   He was aware that the worthy clergyman would highly disapprove of an intimacy
with such extremely unorthodox persons,
and he therefore thought it prudent not to
touch on the subject.   He was anxious
nevertheless to see the chief Druid again,
and to acquaint him with the new and unexpected direction which events had taken,

and he therefore waited the approach of the appointed evening with some impatience. He was not kept waiting long, for the man whom he sought came almost immediately, and listened attentively to Frederick's narrative.

"If you had told me three days ago that it was your intention to break off the engagement I should have advised you to wait," he said; "but under the circumstances you could hardly help taking this course; and I do not apprehend any ill results from it. Mrs. Emmerson has too much food for thought and scope for action to be able to form any designs against Miss Hughes just at present, and before she can do so she and I will have a personal interview on this and other business."

"You are jesting," cried Frederick; "you do not surely mean to call upon her yourself?"

"Certainly I do," he replied; "but as you do not understand Mrs. Emmerson's affairs I can hardly explain them to you now. I

came to meet you to-night for another purpose. For some time I have noticed increasing indications of the interest which you
take in our religion, and I wished to know
whether this be the case, and if so, whether
you would like to be admitted into the rights
and privileges of the Druids."

" I can scarcely reply," answered Frederick; " I have not, I confess, thought of
the matter in this light, but if a belief in
the Druidical religion as a religion is a
necessary qualification, I fear that I am not
a suitable candidate, for I have long ago
lost all faith in forms of creed and systems
of religious teaching."

"I am indeed sorry to hear it," replied
the Druid, gravely; "it would be much
more pleasing to me if you professed your
adherence to the most intolerant form of
religion that ever existed, than to believe
that you deliberately disclaimed all creeds
and faiths. There is no man so utterly
miserable as an unbeliever. It is better far
to cling to the wildest superstition ever

devised by men or devils than to cast aside
faith entirely."

"You have mistaken what I wish to
imply," observed Frederick. "I believe as
firmly as you do in the existence of the Deity.
I go even further, and believe in the Christian writings, which we call the Bible; but I
decline to pledge myself to any sect, or to
bind myself down by any professions whatever. And as for joining yours, I have said
that I believe in Christianity, and therefore
I cannot believe in Druidism. That you
may have a treasure and wealth of learned
lore which has been lost to us is quite probable, and that by leading secluded and
studious lives you may have penetrated
secrets inaccessible to us; but even if this
be the case it cannot change my convic-
tions. But why should we discuss a point
which is only calculated to create ill-feeling
between us?" he asked, as he noticed the
pained expression of the Druid's face; "let
us continue to be friends, mutually respecting each other's opinions. Shall it be so?"

"With all my heart, if it must be so," replied the Druid; "but I still regret that you are not more favourably impressed with our creed. You are right in supposing that we are acquainted with secrets unknown to your philosophers; and if you have no objection to walk two or three miles to-night, I can give you some slight evidence of our power, though not, I assure you, for the purpose of converting you. My object is merely to prove to you that we have something more than vain assertions to build upon. Will you come?"

"I shall be delighted," said Frederick, "and as for my joining the order or the brotherhood, we will speak no more about it."

With this understanding they set forth on their journey. Striking out eastwards they advanced towards a part of the hills of which Frederick knew nothing, and after about an hour's hard walking they drew near a small copse of trees—the only trees they had seen during their walk. Evidently this was the spot to which they were bent, for the Druid paused before entering the trees, and turned to his companion.

" This wood is reputed to be haunted, and with some reason, as you will presently discover," he said; " and as the ground within has been tunnelled under in the olden times it is rather unsafe in some places, so that you must follow in my footsteps as closely as possible."

The plantation, if it might be called so, was inclosed by a hedge, but they had no difficulty in overcoming this obstacle, and they quickly found themselves beneath the deep shadows of the trees. The ground was indeed very insecure, and seemed almost ready to give way beneath them, but relying on the Druid's guidance he followed him as closely as possible.

They came at length to a small open glade near the centre, and here his guide knelt down and applied his eye for some time to what seemed to be the bare earth. Rising up again he bade Frederick to do so also, and he obeyed the injunction, although he was at a loss to understand the purport of burying his face in the grass and earth wet with the falling dew.

"What do you see?" asked the Druid.

"Nothing," replied Frederick.

"Remain there, nevertheless, and whatever you may see, remember that you are not to utter one word until I give you permission."

He was perfectly silent after this injunction, and whatever the nature of his incantations might be, the Englishman stretched out upon the grass could hear nothing. Presently, however, the apparent darkness before his eyes gradually rolled away and he saw a deep grey mist beneath him, upon which he seemed to be gazing through a number of small openings in the ground. Gradually again the mist vanished and he beheld a large vaulted chamber, lighted he knew not how, but of which every corner was visible. Around it sat twenty skeletons,—grinning, hideous skeletons; but,

nevertheless, they appeared to be endowed
with life, for they moved in their seats, and
he could almost fancy that he could see
their jaws shaking. They wagged their
heads at one another, and finally some of
them stood up and appeared to be convers-
ing with one another in small groups.

Around this room were strewn tattered
flags with the national emblem, the Red
Dragon, and daggers and sheaves of
arrows, with a few rude bows, lay upon the
ground. The living skeletons seemed, at
length, to have arrived at some conclusion,
for they sat down again, and hung their
heads upon their fleshless hands as if in
deep despondency. Then the mist concealed the hideous assembly once more,
and in a few moments profound darkness
only met his eye.

"You may rise now," said the Druid;
"you have seen to-night a sight which
many have longed in vain to witness.
What do you suppose that gathering was?"

"I dare not guess, unless they were

some unfortunate persons who lie unburied here."

"You are partly right," he said; "they were Welsh chieftains six hundred years ago, and were pursued by the English until they took refuge in a cave beneath this wood. Their pursuers tracked them to this spot, and not daring to venture down below they kept watch over the entrance until the unhappy chiefs were starved to death. That is a specimen of English justice—of the treatment which we experienced in those days, and can you wonder then that their spirits still haunt the spot, and that they cannot slumber peacefully?"

"But can you not gain access to the cave?"

"Certainly we can—see here," and he pushed aside the brushwood in a spot where it seemed to be unusually dense, and disclosed to view a dark opening, "that is the entrance to the vault of death, although the passage is not now open. A living foot has not entered that sepulchre since the day when those devoted men uttered their last groan, but *I have been there—I have conversed with the heroes in spirit.*"

"Will you not let me witness this crowning proof of your powers?" asked Frederick, naturally anxious to penetrate the mystery, if possible.

"Not to-night," he replied, with a slight shiver, "I cannot free my spirit from its bodily trammels at will, and to-night my soul is fettered." They returned (almost in silence) in the direction from whence they came, and here the Druid bade him good-night. "If ever you wish to speak to me you have only to come here at the same hour as upon this evening and I shall be present," he said, as they parted.

# CHAPTER X.

## MR. DARBY DEPARTS.

FREDERICK was busily employed next morning in writing some letters when the servant announced Mr. Darby. Frederick jumped up in some surprise, for his reminiscences connected with the reverend gentleman were not altogether agreeable, and he was therefore astonished that he should call upon him.

"You are wondering, sir, why I have ventured to intrude upon you," he said, very humbly, as he advanced into the room, "but I have determined upon leaving Glynarth for a charge in England, and I could not go away without asking you to pardon the injury I have done you."

Frederick was touched by the poor philosopher's evident agitation, and he relented in a moment.

"My dear sir, do not speak of it again," he said, very warmly; "it was a most unfortunate business, but it has been righted at last, and now we are all good friends again."

And the two men who had once been bitter foes shook hands cordially.

"I am really sorry that you are going away," said Frederick, sincerely. "I have heard nothing of your intention to do so."

"No; my congregation worshipped at some distance from Glynarth, and but few of its members resided here," he replied, "and my movements are too insignificant to be gossipped about, especially after Mrs. Emmerson's patronage was withdrawn."

"Why was it withdrawn?" asked Frederick, who of late had heard nothing whatever of the minister or his proceedings.

"Because she seemed to think that by some means or other I ought to have married Miss Hughes, even if I had to carry her to church by force; and she took me to task severely for what she termed my clumsiness. I had endured a good deal from her in silence, but I could not submit to this fresh insult, and therefore I spoke very plainly to her.

"And so you quarrelled? Well, perhaps it is better for your own sake that it should be so," observed Frederick.

"I agree with you," replied Mr. Darby; "my position here would become in time an unpleasant one, unless I found means of appeasing her, and I could only do so by lending myself again to her schemes. In various ways she has tried to persecute me, for it is a remarkable fact, sir, in human nature, that when a woman once grasps an idea, be it true or false, she clings to it more tenaciously than any other animal in creation; and I use the word animal here in its broad, philosophical sense. Now, Mrs. Emmerson is a most energetic woman, as you are aware, and is possessed of a

large amount of what I may call *vis viva*,
or accumulated energy, as the mechanicians
have named it; and when she imbibes a
prejudice against any one, she will manage
to make his or her life intolerable."

"If she were removed from Glynarth,
would your fears be dispelled?" asked
Frederick.

"Yes; but even in that case I would not
stay," he replied. "Why should I remain
here to witness a happiness which can only
fill me with grief? No, I must go."

His voice shook a little, notwithstanding
his efforts to control it.

"There is but one request which I wish
to make to you," he continued, "and it
is this: I should go away from here in
a happier state of mind if *she* wished me
God speed. She has forgiven me already;
but, under the circumstances, as your
engagement has been renewed, I thought
it due to you to ask you to accompany
me."

"I am sure that you would rather go

alone, Mr. Darby," replied Frederick; "and if it be any satisfaction to you, I give you my full permission to call upon her. I can trust both her and you."

And the minister thanked him from the bottom of his heart, and then prepared to go.

"If ever I can be of any service to you, Mr. Darby, you have only to command me," said Frederick. "I sincerely hope that in your new sphere you will be very happy, and that we shall hear before long of your marriage with one of my fair countrywomen."

"No, it will be a long time before you hear that," he said, shaking his head mournfully; "but I am none the less grateful for your good wishes. I leave Glynarth to-morrow, and so good-bye."

Frederick felt almost as sorry to part with him as if he had been an old and intimate friend, and tears stood in the minister's eyes.

"I shall be glad to hear of your success,"

he said, as they separated finally; "my
bride and myself will always retain kindly
memories of you."

Why, indeed, should Frederick be angry
with him? It is true that he had been
a party to Mrs. Emmerson's scheme for
blighting Annie's happiness, but the great-
ness of his love for her almost excused
that to Frederick's mind. It is sweet to
feel that other men prize the treasure
which you have won when it is secure in
your keeping, and so Mr. Darby's faults
were forgotten, and his virtues only remembered.

He went to the Glyn that afternoon
for the purpose of bidding Annie farewell,
and as she had heard nothing of his approaching departure, she was rather surprised to see him.

"I have just called upon Mr. Danvers,"
he said, "and I told him that I intended
coming here to bid you good-bye, Miss
Hughes, for I am going away from Glynarth."

"Indeed! This is rather a sudden resolve, is it not?" she said.

"Not very," he replied: "it is a remarkable fact that when a man finds the course of events setting against him, he feels desirous to change his locality and his field of operations, and as I have not been very happy or very successful here lately, I have determined upon seeking 'fresh fields and pastures new'—as the poet observes."

There was nothing more than a friendly parting between them. Annie had suffered much from his co-operation with Mrs. Emmerson's plans, and, though she had quite forgiven him, she could not overcome a certain feeling of dislike for him. But still she wished him every success and happiness, and the minister went away, feeling that the only chapter of romance in his life was closed for ever.

When he arrived at his lodgings he found a parcel of books, which had been sent by Frederick as a farewell gift, and his success-

ful rival's generosity touched him deeply.
He left Glynarth two days afterwards, and
all that was ever heard of him afterwards
was that, after retaining the charge of his
new congregation for some two years, his
health failed, and after a long and weary
illness he died.

## CHAPTER XI.

### THE WAY TO THE SPIRIT LAND.

ANNIE had never visited the Lodge, and had, in fact, never seen the interior of her lover's residence; but yielding to his earnest invitation, she was one day shown over it. The tidings of the renewed engagement between them had been quickly noised abroad; and although Annie's friendless position, without any near relative to advise her, was rather a peculiar one, this visit to the place which would soon be her home was generally approved of by the village authorities on the etiquette of love, court-ship, and marriage.

She had, however, bethought herself of an old lady who stood in some relation to her—an aunt, she believed, though she was not quite certain—and this lady, Mrs. Edwards, who resided in the adjoining county, had graciously accepted an invitation to take up her abode at the Glyn until after the wedding, and to preside over the details and arrangements connected with that interesting event, which was to come off in another month.

In the mornings and evenings Mrs. Edwards and herself were busily occupied with the wedding *trousseau*, and if the courtship had been rather opposed to the orthodox fashion approved of by city *belles*, the bride's outfit was formed on much the same principle. There were no frequent visits to Regent Street or Oxford Street possible, and no Parisian *modiste* was called in to superintend the important work. The resources of the village draper were indeed found to be too limited, and the aunt and niece (for, of course, if Annie was ready to accept her as her aunt, we are bound to do so likewise, although the relationships of the Welsh are extremely intricate, and would puzzle Sir Bernard Burke himself) paid a two days' visit to Abernant, returning home well laden with all kinds of bewildering fabrics.

As for Frederick, he insisted upon spending nearly every afternoon in her society, and the dear old lady, who played the part of propriety, had a convenient fondness for a siesta on these occasions, by which she gained Frederick's undying gratitude. During these hours of bliss they walked together, gardened together, drove out on sunny days, and stayed at the Glyn in loving converse on cloudy ones, and sometimes their conversation referred to serious events which occurred bearing upon Mrs. Emmerson and her fortunes. But we must not anticipate.

On rainy days Frederick had to remain in-doors, smoking himself into a state of oriental stolidity; and on such afternoons the purple and fine linen at the Glyn, which was scrupulously preserved from his sight, was brought out, and the ladies pushed on their millinery operations.

A week had passed away since Frederick's last visit to the Druid, and still there was no indication of any operations against Mrs. Emmerson. Filled with a desire to see him again, he repaired one night to the old trysting place, and waited long for the Druid's arrival; and at length, after a considerable delay, he came.

"I have kept you waiting," he said, "but my attention was occupied with serious business, and I could not postpone it."

"Do not let me detain you then," said Frederick, quickly; "I had no particular reason for coming here to-night, so that I should be sorry to take you away from your business."

"It is over now and concluded," he said, waving his hand; "and as for your reason in coming here to-night, I believe that I can guess it. You wish to know why we are still leaving Mrs. Emmerson in possession?"

"You are right. I confess that I expected some decisive step on your part before this."

"We are possessed of full information respecting her and her movements," the Druid said; "and we think it best to allow matters to take their course, because she herself will precipitate matters. To-morrow morning she leaves for London on some business, the nature of which I am fully aware of, and when she returns there will be fresh food for scandal in Glynarth."

"Of course I cannot comprehend your plan of operations, but I have no doubt that you are acting wisely," Frederick said; "still, unless I were certain that Mrs. Emmerson has forfeited all claims to kindly consideration, I, for one, would not plot as it were against her thus."

"She is the guiltiest of all that guilty house," said the Druid, fiercely, "and her punishment will be heavier than that of the rest. But let us enter."

He led the way into the cave, and here

Frederick saw Sian sitting over a peat fire.
The old woman paid no attention to his
entrance, but kept her eyes steadily fixed
upon the stockings which she was knitting.

From here they sought the chapel, where
the fire was still burning as before on the
altar.

"I have brought you in here to-night,"
said the Druid, in a low voice, "because it
is a night upon which I hold communion
with the sages of our faith who have passed
away. Whatever you may see, do not be
alarmed, but remain perfectly still, feeling
sure that when our conference is at an end,
my spirit will return."

He walked up to the altar, leaving
Frederick in a state of great perplexity as
to what his precise meaning was, and he
watched his movements therefore with
some curiosity. Seating himself in a
chair of old oak, which stood near the
altar, the Druid fixed his eyes steadily
upon the blue flames, and with folded
arms seemed to wait in silence the com-

ing of the spirits whom he had spoken of. Gradually a change came over his face. The slight colour of his cheeks gave way to a deadly pallor, the lips were tightly compressed, and the eyes seemed to dilate as if in horror at some hideous apparition in the flame. One by one every sign of life faded away, and at length, in less than ten minutes after their entrance into the chapel, he was to all appearances a dead man.

Frederick could not withstand the temptation to examine him, in spite of his injunction to the contrary. The eyes were glassy, and a film seemed to have overspread them; the muscles were as stiff and rigid as iron; and taking a feather from a bundle which happened to lie near, he held it to his lips, but there was not even the faintest indication of life; and as he thought of his own position there, alone with an apparently lifeless man, he began to feel serious alarm.

He drew forth his watch and counted the minutes as they sped away. Seven had

elapsed, and another was on the wing, when
he fancied that the cloud which shadowed
the depth of the Druid's eyes had passed
away, the stiffened limbs gradually relaxed,
and the faint flutter of the eyelids was a
welcome sign that the suspended circulation
was again flowing in its course. With a
deep sigh he closed his eyes, and the spell
was broken, for he stood up, though he
almost tottered with faintness.

"The trance is over," he said; "let me
lean on your arm, and we will leave this
place, which is thronged by phantom
forms."

Nothing loth, Frederick accompanied him,
until they stood again in the open air, and
the fresh, cool breeze revived the Druid.

"You have seen what no alien has ever
been allowed to witness before," he said,—
"the highest effort of the human will, and
the greatest triumph over the grossness of
our nature."

"Then your spirit had really left your
body?" said Frederick, anxious to learn

something as to the sensation which he must have experienced.

"As really as the spirits of the dead in the Glynarth churchyard," he replied; "and it was away from its earthly tenement for a longer period than I have ever experienced before. Another minute, and the suspended life-fluid would never have flowed again."

"Was it a painful sensation thus to shake off the prison which enfolds the soul?" asked his listener; "and what is to be met with on the borders of the spirit land?"

"That it is a painful sensation you cannot doubt," he said, "although the pain decreases at every successive effort; but the scenes which I have witnessed I dare not portray. You do not understand the language of that realm, and its thoughts would be incomprehensible to you. But we must part now. When we meet again, the last act in the tragedy will have begun. Farewell."

He strode away, and disappeared again in the recesses of the caves, and Frederick returned to his home. The lights were glimmering in many a villager's home as he passed, and he saw many a group of happy faces sitting round the fire. He thought with pleasure that the time was not far distant now when he too would have a home of his own, brightened by the presence of a loved one ; and the prospect was indeed a very fair and sunny one.

## CHAPTER XII.

MRS. EMMERSON IS TRIUMPHANT.

THE mistress of Montressor House sat in her boudoir one evening, busily engaged in searching for some papers which she intended to take with her to London on the following day.   Her affairs were indeed fast becoming desperate, for her home expenditure had increased since her second marriage, and the constant drain upon her resources which the demands of Edmund Montressor created tended still further to embarrass and complicate her finances.   She had determined, however, to put an end to all this now, though how she was to accomplish this very desirable object was by no means clear.

Her case was indeed a very hopeless one.
From first to last she had been playing a
losing game, and there had not been even
the semblance of success which very frequently attends evil-doers.   Her intended
victims had all escaped from her toils, and
she herself had married a man for perform-
ing a deed which was not completed after
all.   And now, in this visit to London, what
could she do, supposing that the mysterious
writer of the many mysterious letters she had
received, proved to be Edmund Montressor?
She had but two resources remaining : the
one was, to endeavour to make some perma-
nent arrangement with him—an arrangement
which his fancy or his necessities might
prompt him at any moment to repudiate ;
the other was, to devise some plan by which
he would be effectually removed from her
path.   She did not shrink from the perpe-
tration of another crime ; but she was perfectly aware that it would be attended with
very much more danger and difficulty in the
midst of a populous city like London, than

on the almost uninhabited mountains of
Wales. On every side innumerable difficulties presented themselves, but she could
not extricate herself from them, except by
wading still deeper into sin.

The fire cast a bright and ruddy glow
upon the hearth, but the woman who sat
before it, filled with anxious thought, heeded
it not. She was thinking of her early days,
when her only cares were speculations as to
how a new dress or a new bonnet could be
procured from her slender salary, and she
could sleep peacefully, with nothing more
serious to disturb her rest than the soft
nothings of the amorous youths to whom
during her waking hours it was her duty to
dispense refreshments. Her ambition had
carried her above and beyond that humble
sphere; and yet at this moment, surrounded
as she was by all the appliances and luxuries
of wealth, she would have given unnumbered
worlds, if they had been hers, to stand again
a girl of twenty behind an hotel bar for
twenty-five pounds a year! To her, as to

many before and after her, wealth had brought nothing but bitterness and disappointment, like Dead Sea fruit becoming ashes in her grasp.  Musing thus, a servant tapped at the door, and announced that an old woman was below who wished to speak with her.

"Who is she?" asked his mistress, sharply, for she was in no mood that evening to listen to the petty troubles of some rheumatic old dame.

"I don't know, ma'am," the servant answered; "but she is very anxious to see you, and says that her business is very important."

"Show her in then," she said, wondering as to who her urgent visitor might be.

The old woman entered, and a wild hope sprang up in Mrs. Emmerson's heart as she recognised Sian,—Sian, with none of the hatred and contempt which had filled her on previous occasions, but humble and subdued.

"Well, Sian, what do you want?" asked

the lady, kindly, and speaking in the Welsh
language. "I did not expect to see you
here, but I am very glad that you have
come. What can I do for you?"

"Well, the truth is, that I am very sorry
for having offended you," said the old
woman, very humbly; "and as I would
like to do anything I can to please you, I
thought I would come and see if you would
like to have those papers we spoke about."

Mrs. Emmerson's heart beat violently as
she heard this offer, and her eyes sparkled
with triumphant glee. Like to have them?
Of course she would, for the victory would
then be entirely hers ; but it was not wise to
allow the old woman to see of what immense
importance these documents were to her,
and accordingly she dissembled a little.

"Well, I certainly should like to have
them," she said; "but as I have been able
to do without them hitherto, they cannot
be of much interest to me. Still, if you
like to give them me, I shall be very much
pleased."

"Yes, but you are rich and I am very poor," said the old woman, with an avaricious gleam in her eye; " and if I give you these papers I shall expect to be paid for them."

"You came here then to drive a bargain?" said Mrs. Emmerson, somewhat undeceived as to the object of her visit.

"Yes, although I hope you will not find my price a high one. What will you give for them?"

"Five pounds," said Mrs. Emmerson.

"Nonsense!" cried Sian, with a derisive laugh. "If you like to give me a hundred you shall have them, but not for a farthing less."

So it was to be a fair and open bargain. The old woman was evidently aware of the value of her possession, and was not to be deceived by the crafty schemer before her. As for Mrs. Emmerson herself, she would have given ten times the amount, if necessary, in order to set her mind at rest for ever.

"It is a great deal of money, Sian," she said, thoughtfully; "and as I do not know what the papers are about I cannot say whether they are worth it; but as you are old and poor, and I am anxious to help you, I will give you the hundred pounds."

"Very good," said the old crone, with a short laugh, which indicated how completely she comprehended Mrs. Emmerson's charitable intentions. "I will go and fetch them."

"Have you not got them with you?" asked the lady, in a tone of surprise.

"Oh, no; for, of course, some one might have robbed me and taken them away by force," she replied, in a significant manner; "and I thought it best to come and settle the matter with you first. I will not be long; and when I bring them I shall expect the money."

"It shall be ready," said Mrs. Emmerson; and the old woman hurried away on her errand.

During her absence Mrs. Emmerson

strode up and down the room, with flushed
cheeks and a wildly beating heart. The
winning cards were in her own hands now,
or soon would be, and she could hurl
defiance at the whole world. The estate
was hers for ever; for these papers she was
certain contained proofs which alone could
establish Edmund Montressor's identity, and
with them every particle of proof in his
favour perished. But suddenly a thought
crossed her brain which allayed her rising
excitement.

"They may be forgeries," she muttered;
"but if they are they must be very cleverly
executed to deceive me. I don't suppose
there is any one about here skilful enough to
execute copies of old documents, and the old
woman would hardly have the impudence to
come and sell them to me, even if they had
been executed. No, I fancy they will be
genuine, if she returns at all."

An hour had elapsed since Sian's departure, and Mrs. Emmerson was becoming
fearful that she had repented of the bargain

which she had just made, when the footman again appeared, and admitted the old
woman.    From beneath a long, tattered
cloak which she wore she produced a bundle of a dusty, yellow appearance, which
Mrs. Emmerson was about to seize, when
Sian drew back.

"The money first," she said; and when
the notes were handed to her she did not
appear to be quite satisfied with them.

"They are good notes," said Mrs.
Emmerson, sharply.

"Very likely, but I would much rather
have it in gold," said Sian, who knew nothing of bank-notes, and not very much
about gold either.

"You don't suppose that I have a hundred pounds in gold in the house, do you?"
exclaimed the lady, impatiently.

"Perhaps you can give me some of it in
gold; and if you wouldn't mind sending
that man downstairs to the shop, he might
get some more changed.    They would
think nothing of it if he went, but if I tried

them they would wonder where I got the money from," observed Sian.

Mrs. Emmerson consented to this arrangement, and from both these sources fifty pounds in gold were procured, which satisfied the old woman, and the papers were delivered up. The village tradesman, who combined the business of grocer, chemist, draper, ironmonger, tobacconist, and flour merchant, dispensed his goods in a very unpretending establishment, but his cash-box was fuller than those of many of his urban brethren, and he was able to send thirty of the fifty pounds.

"Now, before you go I want to understand clearly how these papers came into your hands," said Mrs. Emmerson.

"The story is soon told," said the old woman. "In the time of your husband's brother I used to wait about the house, and he often saw me and spoke to me. He found out that I belonged to the Druids, and he often questioned me about them; and I think that he afterwards tried to become

one of us, though I don't think he succeeded.
He had married a weak, puny child, for
whom he did not care much; and after they
had been married three years, and a son
was born, he fell in love with Mrs. Hughes,
of the Glyn, and they ran away, taking the
child with them, a loss which killed its
mother very soon; and I believe that he
took it away because he knew that it would
kill her, for he was a cruel and hard-hearted
man. The night on which they started, he
came to me and brought those papers with
him.

"'I am going away to-night, Sian,' he
said, 'and it may be some years before I
come back; and if anything should happen
to me I should like my son to fill my place
—and to fill it better than I have done,' and
his voice trembled a little. 'In this packet
are papers which prove his claim to the
estate,' he went on,—'papers which might be
lost in the wandering life which I shall have
to lead, and I want you to take them to the
chief Druid, who must never give them up

until some one claims them, bearing a letter from me. Will you do this, Sian?' I promised, and after some more conversation he went away, and the next day we heard that he had gone away, taking Mrs. Hughes and his son with him; and in two months after his departure his wife died of a broken heart."

" Yes, yes; I have heard of all that," said Mrs. Emmerson; "and as you have nothing more to tell me you can go."

She was impatient to open the precious packet, and before doing so she must dismiss the old woman.

" I will take care of them, Sian, you may depend upon that," she said; "and if you should want my help at all I will always be ready to give it you."

She rang the bell, and the footman appeared.

" Take Sian into the kitchen," she said, " and see that she has some refreshment."

Nothing loth, the old woman followed him, and feasted more sumptuously than she

had done for a long time. The servants
tried in vain to discover the errand which
had brought her there, for she refused to
answer any questions on the subject; and
after her meal was over she went away.

"It is spoiling the Philistines," she muttered, in Welsh; "but what would the chief
Druid say if he knew of to-night's work?"

The reflection was rather enigmatical, but
it would be safe to conclude that if he had
suspected treachery in her, her prospects
would be neither bright nor comfortable.

In her own room Mrs. Emmerson was
breaking the seals with hands trembling with
eagerness.

"I understand this affair at last," she
muttered. "He thought that amongst
these people the papers would be safe, and
he went away to enjoy life for a time with
the woman he had enticed from her home.
The nurse found out the secret, perhaps;
or in any case thought that he would pay
a high ransom for his son; but death must
have overtaken him before he could do so,

and then the same fate overtook the woman. The gap between her death and the son's arrival in England I cannot fill up; and it matters nothing to me, nor the fate of the woman he carried away. She is unworthy of a moment's consideration."

And yet that poor unfortunate woman, whose only sin was that of loving a man too fondly—a man who ought to have been nothing to her—was far purer, and less stained with evil, than she who dismissed her memory with such contempt and indifference. She had sacrificed honour and comfort—perhaps even life itself—for the object of her love; and the other had sacrificed her honour, and, so far as she was able, the life and happiness of more than one unoffending victim, and that for the sake of the gold which she loved too well —the gold for which she had bartered her very soul. And yet she regarded herself as immeasurably superior to the woman who had sinned and suffered for love alone.

The packet lay open before her. It con-

tained several papers, which she perused
very carefully.   In the first place, there was
a certificate of a marriage between Edmund
Montressor the father and Alice Durant,
celebrated in a Yorkshire church.   Then
there was a baptismal certificate of Edmund
Montressor the son, and a full statement of
the circumstances of the flight.   Finally,
there was the last will and testament of the
said Edmund Montressor the elder, in which
he bequeathed the whole of his personal and
other property to his wife Alice, to be held
by her during her life, after which it was to
descend to their son.   He appeared to have
made no provision for the companion of his
flight; but, as it was known that he had
carried away with him a very large sum, the
accumulated savings of many frugal pre-
decessors, this was not very surprising.
Mrs. Emmerson was quite satisfied with
these documents.   She had never enter-
tained a real doubt as to the justice of her
nephew's claim; but she was not prepared
for such complete evidence.   With the

destruction of these proofs, however, his claim was over, for it was by no means probable that he would be able to procure fresh proofs sufficiently strong to establish his claim.

"I forgot to ask her why the packet was not delivered to the chief Druid, as she called him," she thought. "I suppose she foresaw the possibility of making a handsome profit out of them at some future time, and therefore retained the secret in her own breast."

She rang the bell again.

"Is Mr. Emmerson in?" she asked, when the servant appeared.

"Yes, ma'am," he replied; "he has just arrived."

"Send him here, and Miss Montressor, too."

Mr. Emmerson had been absent the whole day at the house of a boon companion, some miles away, a soft-headed farmer, who steeped the small amount of brains he possessed in drink very frequently, and who

would have been ruined long before but for
an industrious and prudent wife.    These
two choice spirits had spent the day in fish-
ing, and in imbibing long and deep pota-
tions, so that he was in a somewhat con-
vivial mood when summoned to his wife's
apartment.    Maria was almost unchanged
in appearance—paler, indeed, but beyond
this showing no traces of her recent sorrows.

"What is the matter, my dear?" asked
Mr. Emmerson, as he came unsteadily into
the room; "somebody left you money?—
yellow papers—dirty covering—all the rest
of it.    What's up?"

"My temper will be presently, unless you
behave yourself," she said, angrily; "you
have been drinking again, I see."

"Only to drown my troubles, my dear,"
he said; "hot weather—great deal on my
mind—mulled ale—what's the matter?"

"These are the papers which you tried to
get from Sian," she said, in a slow, impressive voice, hoping that the surprise
would do much to render him sober; and she

was right, for he sprang from his seat as clear-headed as if he had swallowed nothing more potent than water.

" My dear, you are a wonderful woman— I always said you were a wonderful woman," he exclaimed ; " how, in the name of all that is marvellous, did you procure them ? "

" Never mind that at present," she said ; " read them."

He did so, and she watched his countenance, which was lighted up with triumph; whilst Maria also glanced over with some curiosity the documents which were of such vital importance to her mother's interests. When he laid them down Mrs. Emmerson took them up, and cast them into the fire.

" Thus perishes the claim which has kept me so long in suspense," she said, watching the flames until every shred of the all-important proofs were reduced to ashes,— " our troubles are at an end ; and now I will tell you how they came into my hands." The story was soon told, and then their future course was determined upon. " I

shall go to London to-morrow as arranged,"
she said; "and I shall refuse to pay this
man a farthing until he produces proofs as
to his identity. He showed you some
papers, did he not?" she asked.

"Yes—I—I think so," he stammered;
"but really I don't remember what they
were about."

"Ah, you were drunk as usual," she
said, bitterly. "I might as well trust a
child as send you. Those papers were
probably forged, and in any case they
cannot establish his case; and then I will
make short work of him."

"You will not—hurt him," said Maria,
timidly.

"Certainly not, you goose," was the
polite reply; "why should I take the trouble
and run the risk of hurting a man who can
do us no harm? His body is safe enough
so far as I am concerned; but he must be
given to understand that he will never receive a farthing more from me."

"Would you like me to come with you?"

asked Maria, who had never been in London, and who longed to escape from Glynarth.

"No, child," replied her mother, with unusual tenderness. "As soon as this business is settled we will go away for a long tour somewhere, but to-morrow I would prefer to go alone."

Mr. Emmerson retired to rest soon afterwards, and Maria followed his example after wishing her mother a pleasant journey.

"I have a foreboding that it will be very far from pleasant," she said, gloomily; "but we will hope for the best."

There was no repose for her that night, for she remained in her own sitting-room, alternately musing and then adding something to the things she was to take with her, until the short summer night began to disappear before the golden streaks of light from the east, and she could hear the servants rising to prepare for her departure. In these solemn hours of solitude what dark and bitter thoughts must have filled her mind! and in spite of her recent serenity there was a strange sinking at her heart which she could not account for and could not drive away.

## CHAPTER XIII.

### IN THE TOILS.

THERE were no farewell words between Mr. and Mrs. Emmerson, for he was supposed to be sleeping soundly; but if she had peeped into his room she would have found him fully dressed, gazing out from behind the heavy curtains on the carriage which was to convey the lady to the nearest railway station. His face was rather pale and agitated too, much more so than might be expected to be the case if he had nothing more than this journey of his wife's to trouble him.

He had, indeed, a great deal more, for on this day his first wife was coming to Glynarth, coming no doubt to unmask him

and to strip him of the ease and wealth
for which he had sinned so deeply. She
was bringing her child too, and he almost
shuddered as he thought of the frightful
disclosures which she could make, and very
probably would make,—how ruthlessly she
would strip him of his brave feathers, and
turn him adrift again as an outcast in the
world. And she would do this because
she loved him, because she could not
endure to see him linked to another, because
she would prefer penury with him rather
than feast alone with gold drawn from the
purse of another. He was well aware of
her fierce ungovernable disposition, and he
fairly trembled as he thought of the consequences which would result, unless he
could prevent her from visiting Glynarth.

He was drifting further and deeper into
the dark sea of crime. It is but seldom
indeed that a man who is guilty of one
misdeed is able to pause there, for new
and urgent necessities are ever springing
up which seem to call for the commission

of some new sin, and thus it was with
Henry Emmerson.   He had become so
habituated to the awful thought of taking
away life that he was but little agitated by
it, even when that life belonged to the
woman he had sworn to love, to the companion of many of his misfortunes, and the
mother of his child.

He breakfasted alone that morning, for
Maria took advantage of her mother's
absence to take her morning meal in her
own room, leaving Mr. Emmerson to his
own reflections.   After breakfast he strolled
out to his favourite nook to smoke a matu-
tinal pipe, and to decide upon his plan of
action.

It was simply this.   When he found that
she would not be dissuaded from her purpose, he had written to her to say that he
would meet her half-way between Glynarth
and the station, which was twelve miles off,
and as she had not the means to procure a
special conveyance, she would be compelled
to perform this part of her journey on foot.

It would be dark when she reached the station, and he calculated that it would be nearly midnight before they met. After this he must depend entirely upon his own ingenuity to take advantage of any opportunity which might present itself for the execution of his design.

Slowly and wearily the hours of that day dragged themselves away, but the evening began at last to cast long shadows of the trees on the paths, and to tinge the distant hills with the golden glory of the setting sun. Why did Henry Emmerson linger long as he watched the labourers returning homewards from their toil, and the small scholars of the village school lingering about the roads, discussing their evening tasks in the first four rules of arithmetic? It was because a deeper shadow than any left by the departing day had settled upon his spirit, and he wondered what would take place before that sun sank again into its western bed, and he could almost fancy that it disappeared in a crimson sea of blood.

He turned at last and went into the
house, where he remained smoking and
drinking brandy until it was quite dark.
Then he proceeded to disguise himself as
well as he could, and arming himself with
a pair of pistols, which he himself had
carefully loaded, he set out on his errand.
Maria was reading a novel in her mother's
sitting-room, and knew nothing of his
departure. Perhaps she would have endeavoured to speak to him if she could
but foresee when she was to see him again.

He walked slowly and leisurely along,
for there was no occasion for haste; the
doomed woman could not have advanced
far on the road to meet him, and he would
prefer that she should meet him within a
few miles of Glynarth, rather than compel
him to walk a long distance home again—
when his work was accomplished.

He had proceeded about five miles, and
still she came not, so he seated himself on
a convenient milestone, and smoked his
pipe in silence. Indeed, there was no

temptation to be otherwise than silent, for his own thoughts were too unpleasant to be dwelt upon, and the awful silence and desolation of the scene chilled even his callous heart.

An hour, perhaps, passed away thus. Once, indeed, he fancied that he saw a light flickering about in the distance, but he concluded that it was either a will-o'-the-wisp, or, what was more probable still, a corpse-candle. He had heard the villagers speak of such things, and he believed that they really existed; but whose death did this portend? Whose but that of the woman he had doomed to death?

At length he heard the sound of footsteps on the road, and, starting up, he hurried to meet the traveller. It was a female, and she recognised him—at least, she called him by name.

"Henry, is that you?" she asked, and he saw that her child was in her arms.

"Yes, I have been waiting here a long time," he said, in softer tones than usual.

It was so easy to be kind to a woman who stood, as it were, on the threshold of eternity.

"Why didn't you come and meet me farther, then?" she asked; "I am so tired."

"Well, it isn't far now, and you will soon be at rest," he said, in a peculiar voice; "it was your own fault, too, that you ever came here. I tried to stop you, but it was no good."

"I wanted to know what you were doing down here," she said, in a suspicious manner. "When I was in the train to-day, at one of the stations, I saw a grand lady on the platform, and she had a great deal of luggage with her. We were changing trains there, too, and so I looked at the cards on her boxes. There was 'Mrs. Emmerson, passenger to London,' on them. Who was she, do you know?"

"How can I tell who everybody through-out the country is, who happens to have my name?" he exclaimed, shuddering, however, as he thought of this strange meeting between the two women; "you are getting very ridiculous and disagreeable. Come on; let us be moving."

She followed him in silence for a few minutes, and then spoke again.

"You have not asked about the baby yet," she said, half reproachfully.

"Oh, I dare say the child is all right," he said, carelessly; "any way, we will have plenty of time to talk over matters when we get to our journey's end."

He was debating with himself whether he should use firearms or not, and finally decided, if possible, not to do so, for he was by no means certain that the surrounding fields and valleys were uninhabited, and a pistol-shot would be heard with great distinctness and force. He had another plan, which he proceeded to put into operation.

"If we go along the road, it is nearly five miles to Glynarth," he said, "but there is a short cut across the fields, which is not more than two. Now, which shall we take?"

Her last chance of baffling his demon hatred was gone when she said :—

"The nearest way, to be sure. Let us make haste, for I am very tired."

He had not offered to carry the child for her, and she would not have allowed him to do so if he had proposed it. There was an undefined fear in her mind, which caused her to press her babe more closely to her breast, as if in fear lest it should be snatched away from her.

There was a pathway, which led abruptly down into the valley from the high road, and he led the way. He knew the locality well, for he had visited it on many previous occasions, and he knew that at some distance there was an opening on to a precipice, which overhung a small lake which lay in the depth of the valley. This was the place where he purposed to execute his design. They were drawing very near to the place, and still she followed him implicitly.

"It is very dark, Henry," she said once.

"Never mind, you will have plenty of

light soon," he said, grimly; and she was conscious of a vague feeling of uneasiness at his reply.

The rock was not more than six or seven feet above the water, and could, therefore, hardly be called a precipice, perhaps, but still it was not pleasant even to contemplate the possibility of falling from its summit into the green, treacherous water beneath, especially as the lake was a deep one, and the banks were steep and difficult.

When they came to the opening in the fence, which led to the rock, he dropped his stick, as it were accidentally, and appeared to be groping about for it.

"Curse the stick!" he muttered; "turn to your right. I will catch you in a moment."

Twenty paces down the pathway was the rock, and the night was so dark, and there was a turn in the path as it jutted on to the rock, that she saw not her danger.

She heard her husband running behind her, just as she came to this turn in the path, and, in another moment, she saw her danger, for the moon burst forth from behind a cloud, and showed her the peril in which she was placed.

" Henry !" she almost screamed, but, ere she could utter another word, with one tremendous push he dashed her into the water below.

For one instant he glanced over, and saw the white, agonized face of the mother, as she still clasped in death her baby in her arms, and turned her eyes to her murderer in a vain appeal for mercy. The pure moonlight streamed down upon her in her death-agony, and bathed the awful scene in its silvery light, but Emmerson waited no longer. Fancying that he heard footsteps, he turned and fled, whilst the phantom footsteps still followed on his track. He did not dare to look back, lest he should see something which would freeze his blood with horror, but still fled on until—until he received a heavy blow from an unknown hand, and he fell senseless on the ground.

\*    \*    \*    \*    \*    \*

Four days had elapsed since Mrs. Emmerson's departure, and now she was on the point of returning home again—to receive strange and perplexing tidings. Mr. Emmerson had disappeared on the morning after her departure, and, although Maria had directed a vigorous search to be made in all the surrounding neighbourhood; though every pool and lake had been dragged, and sleepy country policemen had been stimulated to activity, and every channel of information had been investigated, no trace of the missing man could be found; and if, from some cause or other, he had fled away, no vestige of his flight could be found. He had disappeared as completely as if he had vanished into thin air.

Maria had never even liked her mother's husband, but she was greatly distressed by his disappearance; and the disquieting rumours which were abroad respecting the Montressor family gained fresh strength from this most mysterious circumstance. Some dread fate seemed, indeed, to be

impending over the family, for just at the
moment when the dark clouds which had
lowered above them were apparently dis-
persed, new misfortunes came to overtake
and perhaps overwhelm them.

Frederick had been most active in the
search, and Mr. Campbell called to sympa-
thize with the distressed young lady in those
few days of misery; but she longed for her
mother's return with that strong desire with
which a weak nature always turns to a
stronger one in hours of perplexity and
distress; and, on the fourth evening, Mrs.
Emmerson came.

Maria stood on the hall-steps awaiting
the carriage-wheels which were so long in
coming, until at length the sound of the
wheels, as they crushed the gravel, reached
her ears. It stopped, and her mother descended with a dark, angry countenance.
Perhaps she guessed, from Maria's face,
that she had something to tell her, for she
said quickly :—

"Not here—come into my room;" and

mother and daughter were shut up together for more than an hour, whilst the servants wondered how she would bear the news.

"Is *he* here?" Mrs. Emmerson asked, as she locked the door behind them.

"No, he disappeared on the night of your departure," said Maria, who was surprised by the unmoved expression of her mother's face.

"I thought as much," she said, fiercely; "I thought the villain would not remain here until his guilt was unmasked. My dear, we have been harbouring a man who has injured us deeply—so deeply, that nothing but his life will be a sufficient penalty. He has robbed and swindled me—*me*, his wife. God help me!" and she sobbed in the intensity of her passion.

Maria was silent, for she was at a loss to know how to soothe the excited woman.

"Let me tell you the miserable story," she said, "and then you will understand my state of mind. When I reached London, I went to the address given in the letters of

this pretended Edmund Montressor, and I
found it to be a small tobacconist's shop.   I
asked for Mr. Montressor, and the man
behind the counter laughed, and said that
there was no such person.   Little suspecting
the nature of the discovery I was about to
make, I bribed the tobacconist to tell me the
whole story, and he said that whenever letters
came for Mr. Montressor, they were sent to
an address in Wales, which he showed me.
It was Emmerson's, at a low public-house in
Abernant, and this man in London posted
his replies to me.   If further proof were
needed, I quickly obtained it, for, on calling
at the bank in Lombard Street, with which
I do business, and making inquiries, I found
that he had an account there in his own
name, which amounted to nearly the total
of the sums he has thus extracted from me.

" Why did you ever marry him, mamma ? "
exclaimed Maria, overwhelmed by these
tidings.

" I cannot tell you, child," she answered ;
" let me proceed with my story.   It struck

me that, knowing himself to be on the brink of discovery, he would abscond, and perhaps take with him his ill-gotten gains, and I, therefore, had an interview with the chief partner, in which I explained to him the state of the case. You can imagine how bitter the humiliation was, but it was absolutely necessary to take this precaution. Fortunately, a marriage settlement had been executed, by which he was unable to touch one penny of my property, and, as this money had been procured by fraud, the banker promised not to honour any cheques he might send in, at least for the present. And then, burning to meet the villain and impostor, I hurried down here, only to find, as I had half expected, that he had made his escape. Tell me all that you know about it."

Maria had but little indeed to communicate, for nothing more than conjectures existed as to his fate. The prevailing impression, indeed, was that he had lost his life by some accident; but Mrs. Emmerson would not accept this view of the case.

"He is alive; I am sure of it," she said, when Maria mentioned these rumours, which she had gathered from the servants; "he was not born to lose his life by an accident, and I only hope that somewhere in this world, or the next, we shall meet again."

It was vain to attempt the hopeless task of soothing her, and as new visions of the disgrace which would follow this flight, for such she believed it to be, presented themselves to her mind, her fury increased.

"Our name is bandied about in every pothouse throughout the country," she exclaimed; "every wretched old hag in Glynarth will exult at our misfortune, and Frederick Danvers, vain fool as he is, will bless the fate which prevented him from allying himself with the daughter of a dishonoured house. But the game is not out yet, and I shall win in the end. I feel as if I could rise from the dust if every mountain in the world were hurled down upon my head."

Misfortunes were crowding around her,

but her spirit rose with every fresh blow.
She was a woman who might have defended
a city against a thousand foes, and could
have laughed in wild triumph as she
perished at last in its flames; a woman
who might have been a shining light in the
world, had she been brought up under
favourable influences.

"What a fool I was ever to trust him,"
she exclaimed, as she strode to and fro in
the room in her agitation; "I ought to have
known that he, of all others, was not
a man to cultivate the domestic virtues
—that, faithless as I knew him to be, he
would be faithless also to me. And yet I
showered benefits upon him. I gave him
everything that money could procure; I
elevated him from being a homeless outcast to a comparatively high place in
the world, and thus he repays me for my
folly!"

The servants were surprised, when she
came forth, how very calm and stern she
was, and how carefully she avoided her

husband's name. They knew not how that
proud heart struggled with the keenest
agony, nor how dark a secret lay concealed
in her breast.

# CHAPTER XIV.

## THE END OF MR. EMMERSON'S CAREER.

EMMERSON lay upon the ground, stunned by the force of the blow dealt by his unknown foe, but not wholly deprived of consciousness. He could see a crowd of dark faces around him, and heard words spoken which he could not understand, and presently rough hands were laid upon him, an' carried on the shoulders of two strong and sturdy mountaineers, he was removed from the scene of the tragedy.

For a time he pretended still to be insensible; but they had not proceeded far when his conductors appeared to suspect the genuineness of his fainting-fit, for they placed him on the ground, and quickly

blindfolded him. This little operation having been performed to their satisfaction, the
procession was reformed, and continued to
move in solemn silence until it came to a
sudden halt, and then the two men who
carried him proceeded alone until they
stopped before a doorway. This was
opened, and the prisoner was placed within
a small cell, and the door was closed
securely upon him.

For many long and weary hours he remained there in a state of fearful suspense,
unable to guess into whose hands he had
fallen, or what his ultimate fate would be.
His wife, he believed, had perished, and if
ever he breathed again the free air of
heaven she would be no longer a stumbling-
block in his path. But would he ever again
stand as a free man in the grounds of Montressor House? The circumstances of his
capture, and the low, small, dark cell in
which he was confined, were not calculated
to still the fears which filled his soul, and
which racked his mind with anguish. A

presentiment, which he could not shake off, clung to him that his race was run, and that the end of his guilty and crime-stained career was at hand; and that end seemed more awful because he could not surmise by whose hand the blow was to be dealt. Some hours passed away thus in doubt and fear; and at length he heard heavy foot-steps without, and the sound of the bolts as they were shot back smote upon his ear. The door was opened, and he saw two stern-faced men without, bearing torches in their hands.

They motioned to him to come forth, and, as he did not immediately obey them, they seized him with no gentle hands, and assisted him to rise to his feet. Then he came forth into the passage—the passage which Frederick Danvers had trodden on several occasions—and they led him into the large hall where the dancing had taken place.

There he found a tribunal awaiting him. On a raised chair sat the chief Druid, and near him stood four others, with whom he occasionally consulted during the trial which took place. Before this chair a table was placed, and at one side Sian sat, whilst opposite the men who were to be the judges, a seat was placed for the prisoner. Torches were fixed in the niches around the room, casting a glaring light on the strange scene.

Emmerson was almost thrust into the seat prepared for him, and his two conductors stood on guard behind him. There were no spectators present; and once, as one of the four men before him left the room for a few minutes, the prisoner saw a sentinel stationed behind the door. To escape from such hands was indeed impossible.

The chief Druid was the first to speak.

"You were arrested a few hours ago," he said, "when in the act of throwing a woman into one of the mountain lakes—a woman who asserts that she is your wife, and you have been brought here to answer this, and another charge, which you shall hear presently."

He spoke in English, and he was the only one in the room, as Emmerson afterwards perceived, who could speak anything besides Welsh.

"What mockery and foolery is this?" asked the prisoner; but his trembling hands and quivering lips were strangely at variance with the boldness of his words; "who are my judges, and who has given them authority to interfere with me or my actions?"

"We are your judges," said the Druid, as he pointed to himself and his colleagues, "and our authority is derived from the power which we possess of executing any sentence we may pass upon you. It is useless to cavil at the tribunal. You will find that your only chance of escape is to justify yourself, if possible.

"I refuse to acknowledge your right to interfere with me, nevertheless," replied the prisoner. "If I have committed any crime, hand me over to the proper authorities, where, at least, I can have a fair trial, in-

stead of arraigning me before a few nameless and unknown vagabonds."

The chief Druid's pale face was perfectly
unmoved, and he betrayed no signs of irri-
tation at the sneering words.

"If you are determined to throw away
your only chance of life the fault is your
own," he said, calmly.   "We have the power
of punishing evil-doers, nameless vagabonds
though we may be ; and you will have no
opportunity for escaping by legal quibbles, as
might be the case in the courts to which you
wish to be transferred.   Call the witnesses."

The last words were spoken in Welsh to
one of the judges, who went to the door,
and spoke to the sentinel.   Returning to
the court—for such it was—he waited with
the rest until four men entered, and ranged
themselves on each side of the table.

"These men watched you as you enticed
your wife—if such she be—to the rock above
the lake, and they saw you hurl her over
into the water.   What have you to say to
this charge ?   Do you admit it ? "

"I admit nothing," the prisoner said. "I refuse to acknowledge your power over me."

"You shall have a practical proof of it before long then," the Druid replied. "This charge, then, we will regard as proved against you—attempted murder— and that of a woman who, according to her own showing, had committed no fault beyond that of trusting you too fully."

"Her own showing!" exclaimed the prisoner. "Is she alive then?"

"That is an admission of your guilt," observed the Druid; "but in order to bring it completely home to you, you shall be confronted with her."

He made a sign, and the woman was brought in, with her child in her arms. She cast an anxious, doubtful look on the prisoner, but did not speak to him.

"Take that seat," the Druid said, pointing to a chair at the table. "And now answer me a few questions. You are this man's wife, are you not?"

" Yes."

" And where did you reside ? "

" In London."

" How long have you been married to him ? "

" For the last eight years."

She spoke in a hesitating manner, as if fearful that she was involving her husband in some danger and trouble.

" And some time ago he left you, did he not ? "

" Yes, and came here."

" Did he tell you what his object was in coming down to so remote a place ? "

" Never ; and he was always very angry if I wrote to him, or tried to find out what he was doing. But why do you ask me these questions? " she asked; and the Druid saw that, unless he was careful, she would refuse to speak. He tried a more crafty policy.

" You were not aware, then, that he was married to another woman here? " he said, slowly and impressively.

" Married to another woman ! Oh, the wicked wretch ! " she exclaimed, quite thrown off her guard. " And because he wanted to stay with her he threw me into the water—the villain ! "

" You say that he threw you into the water. You are quite certain that it was he who pushed you in ? "

" Of course I am. Who else could have done it ? "

" Miserable woman, you have killed me ! " exclaimed the prisoner, starting from his seat, into which, however, he was quickly thrust by his watchful guards.

His wife stared on the chief Druid with mingled alarm and perplexity.

"What have I said ? What are you going to do to him ? "

The Druid did not answer her.

" Take her away," he said, in Welsh, to the men who had been brought in first as witnesses, and they forced her from the room in spite of her struggles to remain there.

" Now, then, prisoner, you have been con-
demned by your wife's own testimony.    You
have been guilty of bigamy ; and you also
stand charged with breaking into the house
of, and endeavouring to rob, a member of
our fraternity—this old woman," indicating
Sian.

Emmerson made no reply.    Awakened to
a sense of his peril, he had covered his face
with his hands, and awaited passively whatever fate was in store for him.

" You tried, by unlawful means, to possess
yourself of papers relating to Edmund
Montressor, and which you must have wished
to obtain in order to destroy all proofs of
his claim," the Druid continued.    " You
have spared no one and nothing in the
pursuit of your evil projects ; and now,
before we pass sentence upon you, what
have you to say in defence of your conduct ? "

" Nothing, except that you are my ac-
cusers and my judges, and that I protest
against these proceedings," Emmerson said,

raising his head, and trying to assume a swaggering air.

"That will avail you nothing," the Druid said; and then, turning to those around him, they consulted together in Welsh.

"Our sentence is," the Druid said, turning to the prisoner, "that you be put to death—in what manner we will decide shortly; but more merciful to you than you were to your wife, two hours will be given you to prepare for death."

"You cannot be serious; this is some farce, very amusing to you perhaps, but it has been carried far enough," the prisoner said.

"It is no farce," was the solemn reply.

"At least give me more than two hours then," he pleaded; "give me a day to prepare for death. Surely you will not refuse me this small boon?"

Again his judges consulted together, and again the Druid spoke.

"We grant your request," he said. "Morning is now breaking. When the coming sun sets you shall die. Take him away."

He made a sign with his hand, and in another minute Emmerson was once more a solitary prisoner in his cell—a prisoner sentenced to death! He had pleaded for delay in the vain hope that, by gaining time, some mode of escape would present itself; but the hours went by slowly, and yet how quickly, to the doomed and dying man—dying in the midst of his days—and not even a glimmer of light entered his mind, clouded as it was by a strong horror and dread of looking forward into that awful, mysterious future which was so near its dawning.

As the day advanced the cell became a little lighter, and, as a forlorn hope, he examined his cell for some possible means of escape, but there was none. It was a small room, dug out from the hill-side, and the door was secured on the outside by heavy bolts. No prisoner in Newgate was ever so safely confined.

" My race is indeed run," he muttered
as he sank again upon his seat; " and this
is the end of my career after all my schemes!
To be put to death by a miserable band
of mountain outlaws! Unless it were all
too real I should think that I was dreaming,
and a frightfully unpleasant dream it is."

Time went by slowly, perhaps, to many
a listless lounger in the world outside, but
with appalling rapidity to that wretched,
cowering, conscience-stricken man, who was
being hurried to an untimely grave. And
how was he to be cut off from life? What
tortures would be inflicted upon him?—or
would he be put to death in one moment,
hardly conscious of the blow before he
crossed the threshold of eternity? These
questions perplexed and tortured him; and
when a man threw open the door, and placed
some food in the cell, he tried to question
him; but as the gaoler could speak nothing
but his native *Cymraeg* he was baffled in
his hope of extracting information from him.

The sun sank into its golden bed amid

the waters of the Cardigan Bay, but the prisoner knew of the fast approaching hour of his doom only by the profound darkness which again filled his cell. He tried to recall some of the simple prayers which he had learned when a child at school, but even his memory seemed to fail him, or else these holier reminiscences of the past had been stamped out by years of sin and vice. He tried to repeat one single verse of a hymn which he remembered, but he could not collect his wandering thoughts to prepare himself, and every receding minute deepened his helplessness and dismay.

Again the sound of the bolts, as they were shot back, came into his ears, and the door was thrown wide open.

"Prisoner, thy hour hath come," the chief Druid said, as two men entered the cell, and proceeded to bind the wretched man's hands.

He submitted passively, for resistance would have been worse than useless. Then

he was led out and brought into the open
air on to the mountain side.

It was quite dark, for the moon was
obscured, and heavy, black clouds were
spread like a pall over the sky. Six men
joined the band here; and, headed by the
chief Druid, they walked in solemn silence
across the same ground as that which they
had traversed on the previous night. Indeed,
it was to the rock from which his wife had
been hurled that Emmerson was now con-
ducted, and then he understood the manner
of his death—*he was to be drowned in the
lake.*

They stood—a grim and silent band, with
a trembling wretch among them—on the
rocks; and now the moon burst forth to
lighten that scene of vengeance. Face
to face with death, the desperation of his
position prompted him to make one last
appeal for mercy.

"Spare me from death," he cried, sinking before the chief Druid, who stood on
the rock, attired in a long white robe, with

a red dragon embroidered upon its breast. "I will pay you any amount you may ask for; but, at least, do not kill me."

"We will not touch your accursed gold— the fruit of your villany," was the reply, and a smile of cold scorn crossed the Druid's pale face as he looked down upon the miserable man; "you have shown no mercy to others—you will receive none from me."

Like the Roman ambassadors before the Carthaginian senate, he had raised with his right hand the folds of his robe, and made a sign to his attendants, and Emmerson was forced to the brink of the rock.

"Spare my life," he cried, piteously, as he turned his face to the Druid—a face frightful to behold, from the intense agony and despair depicted in it; "do anything with me, but let me live."

The Druid let fall the folds of his robe, and the prisoner was hurled into the lake below. He rose three times to the surface, and then, with a last howl of despair, he sank to rise no more. The cold, dark waters closed above their victim, and when the last ripple had disappeared from its surface the white-robed Druid turned, and entered his mountain stronghold again.

## CHAPTER XV.

### MRS. MONTRESSOR'S FINAL DEFEAT.

MRS. MONTRESSOR—for such we must now call her, and indeed she had no real right at any time to the name of the man who had perished in the hill-side lake—was unusually depressed and despondent, although she could assign no cause for the lowness of spirits which she could not shake off. Even in the hour of her supposed triumph an uncomfortable presentiment haunted her, that the golden fruit of so many dark schemes and intrigues was to become dust and ashes in her grasp.

Maria too was very unhappy and miserable. She had allowed herself to drift so completely into day-dreaming of the happi-

ness that was in store for her—the bliss
that was never to be realized—that the
rude awakening crushed for the time every
hope and every pleasure in life, and to her
young spirit sorrow was the more difficult
to bear, because she knew not by sad experience how full the world is of blighted
hopes and unaccomplished wishes—how
constantly everyone's life is overshadowed
by trouble and darkness.

And thus matters stood at Montressor
House on the day when the pride and
power of Mrs. Montressor received its
final blow. The lady of the house was
engaged in writing letters when visitors
were announced — visitors who followed
closely behind the footman, and who were
in Mrs. Montressor's presence before she
could rise to receive them.

There was the chief Druid and the verit-
able Mrs. Emmerson, accompanied by a
young man, whom Mrs. Montressor had
seen once before, lying cold and motion-
less on the highway, apparently with the

ashen hue of death upon his face—a young man whose portrait she had in her possession, and whose claim to his ancestral lands she had, as she believed, entirely destroyed.

They came in the broad daylight, when the sun was high in the heavens, and there was no secrecy connected with their visit. They came openly to attack their enemy in her fortress, and she accepted the issue, and nerved herself for the struggle.

"To what am I indebted for this unexpected visit?" she asked, in her most freezing tones.

"To a determination to do justice, and to wrest from your hands power which you have misused, madam," the Druid said; "and in order that you may the better understand our business, let me introduce my companions—this is Mrs. Emmerson."

"What folly is this, sir?" she asked, angrily; "how can she be Mrs. Emmerson?"

"She is the lawful wife of Henry Emmerson; and if he were here to answer for himself, he would be compelled to admit it," was the grave reply. "You were his second wife, married during the lifetime of the first."

This was a heavy and unexpected blow, and, reluctant as she was to believe it, a conviction of the truth of the stranger's statement took possession of her mind instantly, although she would have died rather than admit it.

"Go on, sir," she said, sneeringly. "I am quite prepared for anything you may say after this; but, of course, you can prove your words?"

"Full proof shall be laid before you directly," the Druid replied; "this gentleman I need hardly introduce, for he is a relative of yours; and from the interest you have recently taken in his movements, you probably know as much of his history as I do."

"I am not acquainted with him, though he may be a relative, as you remark. Pray what is your business with me, sir?"

She addressed herself directly to the young man, but the Druid replied for him.

"He has come, madam, to claim his father's estate, and other property—property which has been wrongfully in your possession for many years."

"That has to be shown," she answered, defiantly; "let him produce his proofs."

"That will be done in another place," replied the young man, speaking for the first time. "I have not come here to show you documents which you would gladly destroy, but merely to advise you, now that resistance is useless, to give up an unavailing struggle."

"And what, may I ask, is your name, sir, since you have found your tongue," she asked.

"Charles Montressor," he replied.

"*Charles* Montressor!" she exclaimed; "and you are, you say, the son of my late brother-in-law?"

"I am; but in order to make the case clear to you, I may as well enter into a short history of myself," he said. "My father, as you know, went away from here, taking Mrs. Hughes and his son Edmund with him. His wife and Mrs. Hughes's husband died within two years after the arrival of the two in the United States, and they were then legally married. Edmund Montressor was stolen away by his nurse, and he died of yellow fever, as well as the woman who had taken him away. I was born soon afterwards, and when my father also died, he bequeathed to me the whole of his property. These are facts, madam, which I am prepared to prove, and apparently they astonish you exceedingly."

He was right; and she was not only astonished beyond measure, but greatly irritated, for she understood fully now the fancied treachery of Sian towards her old master's son. It was a mere plan for selling worthless and valueless papers. The game was indeed played out, and Mrs. Montressor decided upon surrendering with as good a grace as possible.

"If this be the truth," she said, more softly, "you are certainly the rightful inheritor, and I will not oppose your claim : but it must be clearly established. You have the necessary certificates, I presume?"

"They are in the hands of my solicitor in London, madam," he replied, coldly ; "and as for withdrawing your opposition, I should feel more disposed to deal kindly with you, but for the deliberate plot which you conceived and executed, so far as you were able, to take away my life."

She started violently, for she had been in hopes that her share in the transaction was unknown to him.

"What do you mean, sir?" she asked, while an angry flush spread over her face.

"We mean, madam, that this gentleman was quite conscious while he lay in the highway, shot by Emmerson acting under your directions," the Druid replied ; "and in that state you came and examined him, in order to be certain that your wicked purpose was accomplished. We are acquainted with the

history of your marriage," he went on,
hazarding a shot, which he saw was an effective one, " and we can hardly be sorry that
a union based upon the blood of a relative
should not have been a happy one."

" And who are you, sir, who have studied
my private affairs so minutely?" she asked,
angrily.

" It will not benefit you to be told my
name," he said, calmly ; " it is enough for
you to know that your plots and plans are all
known to me, and that your career at Glynarth is at an end."

" I am willing to allow you a week to
make the necessary preparations for leaving
here," Charles Montressor said ; " and in
the meantime I shall remain here to protect
my own interests—that is, unless you are
disposed to dispute my rights, and to have
the whole question tried in a law court, in
which case the story of my sufferings and of
your instrumentality in them will be made
known."

" I shall not dispute it," she said, briefly.

"In that case, then, our business here is at an end," said the Druid, rising; "and I will leave you," he said, addressing Charles.

Both the young men left the room together, that their leave-taking might be unobserved. Charles Montressor owed a heavy debt of gratitude to his mysterious friend, for, through his instrumentality he had been carried away from the highway on the night of the would-be murder, and his wounds carefully attended to until he recovered, and he had received considerable help from him in the establishment of his claim.

"From this hour our intimacy is at an end," the Druid said; "now that justice has triumphed, my work is accomplished; and I return to my mountain life, and to that privacy and study which I have too long abandoned."

"But surely I shall see you again?" Charles Montressor asked.

"Sometimes, perhaps, but not often,"

the Druid said ; " our pursuits and hopes in
life are distinct and different, and we part
here."

With a warm pressure of each other's
hands, they parted, and the Druid strode
slowly away.   The two women were engaged, during these few minutes, in conversation in the room from which the two
young men had just issued.

"Are you his wife?" Mrs. Montressor
demanded, rising, and standing before her
rival, if such she were.

"Yes, ma'am," she replied ; "we were
married eight years ago.  I am very sorry
that he took you in."

To be pitied by this poor and friendless
woman was more than Mrs. Montressor's
pride could endure.

"I want none of your sympathy," she
said, harshly ; "if ever I find *him* he shall
suffer for his villany ; but I will never hear
his name again from anyone else."

And as they sat there, ignorant of his
fate, Henry Emmerson was sleeping in a

grave amongst the hills, dug for him by the Druids, and for ever removed from the reach of Mrs. Montressor's vengeance.

# CHAPTER XVI.

## "ALL'S WELL THAT ENDS WELL."

THE news of Mrs. Montressor's fall, and the arrival of a new master, who was in some measure one of themselves, created considerable excitement, in a small way, in the village. Mr. Campbell heard it, amongst the first, and he called at the Lodge to give a full and true account of the circumstances to Frederick, who saw, in this startling change in Mrs. Montressor's fortunes, a new proof of the Druid's power. Mrs. Montressor and her daughter left Glynarth on the following day, and the new owner made them an allowance of three hundred a year, which enabled them to live in tolerable style at a tenth-rate English watering-place.

Maria eventually succeeded in fascinating a young and susceptible curate, who was eager to share his small income with a wife, and Mrs. Montressor herself has had more than one offer from retired officers, and other gentlemen of mature age—offers which she has persistently declined. Her declining years are miserable, and darkened by a remorse which she cannot shake off, and filled with bitter and unavailing regrets.

It is pleasant to turn our steps to Glynarth once more. Charles Montressor paid an early visit to the Glyn, to his half-sister Annie, and he insisted that the wedding should be celebrated at his residence. The marriage-day was a bright and unclouded one in summer. The village scholars had received a holiday in honour of the occasion, and the schoolroom had been tastefully decorated with evergreens and mottoes, although these last were not very appropriate, for they belonged mostly to the two local friendly societies, and had been pressed

into the service because they were handsome, and had a good effect. In this abode
of learning unlimited beer was dispensed in
the morning, and equally unlimited tea and
currant-loaf in the afternoon, to all comers.
The ceremony took place at the sea-side
church, where Annie had so long been an
active member. Charles Montressor's carriage conveyed the bride and her bridesmaids
to the church, and that gentleman himself
acted as groomsman. Mrs. Edwards was
there, rather uncertain as to whether she
should laugh or cry, but finally decided upon
doing neither; but, taking a mean between
the two extremes, she was very cheerful and
very happy.

The little church, with its bare walls, presented a more lively appearance than it had
ever done before, for it was crowded by
villagers who had come from Glynarth and
all the surrounding neighbourhood; and
Mr. Campbell read the service. His voice
was a little unsteady at times, although no
one noticed it. Perhaps the young clergy-

man envied Frederick his happiness—
perhaps — but we will not inquire too
closely into his private affairs.

And now, for the satisfaction of my lady
readers, I must describe the bride's dress.
She was attired in a white grenadine dress
over white silk, with a veil, and a wreath
formed of white roses and orange-blossoms,
and these excited the unbounded admiration
of the rustic and envious belles who had
honoured the ceremony with their presence.
The three bridesmaids wore white dresses,
trimmed with blue forget-me-nots, and cor-
responding wreaths; and to each of them
Frederick had presented massive gold
lockets. But the centre figure in the
group, after all, was the bride. Her sweet,
lovely face was touchingly beautiful—half
smiling, half-sad—and yet the words which
united her to the man of her choice were
spoken in a low, but brave and hopeful
voice.

Mr. Charles Montressor was not, I regret
to say, a very efficient groomsman, for he

managed to upset the parochial inkstand in
signing the register, and was in a perpetual
state of anxiety lest he might be neglecting
his duties, or doing something positively
wrong and contrary to Glynarth etiquette.
He, however, excused himself subsequently,
on the ground that he had never undertaken
such responsible duties before, and, on the
whole, the ceremony passed off very
smoothly. As the newly-married couple
left the church, a gun was fired above their
heads, in accordance with a custom prevalent in the neighbourhood. The villagers
then betook themselves—the young ones to
unlimited fun and flirtation, the old ones
to copious tea-drinking and gossip. The
wedding-breakfast was a great success, for,
the most important part of the proceedings
being over, every one felt more at ease;
and Charles Montressor's speech was
greatly applauded. When the breakfast
was at an end, Annie retired to assume her
travelling attire, and when she quickly made
her appearance again, in a poplin dress of

silver grey, with appropriate gloves and
veil, the carriage was at the door, and they
drove off amid a shower of old boots and
slippers, which had been diligently collected
by the servants from various sources; and
one of these missiles came in contact with
the grave and dignified coachman's nose,
and ruffled the even tenor of that gentleman's feelings.

They spent their honeymoon in Switzer-
land and Italy, and then returned to Glynarth, where Annie still assists Mr. Campbell
in the parish, and Frederick has become a
most exemplary Churchman, much to the
vicar's satisfaction. Charles Montressor
married an English lady some years afterwards, and he provided for Henry Emmerson's unfortunate widow. As for the Druid,
he still clings to a dying creed, and he is
regarded with veneration by the whole
country-side; but Frederick and he but
rarely cross each other's paths.

And thus we leave sweet Annie Hughes
—but Annie Hughes no longer. Happy in

her husband's love, and with children's merry voices prattling in her home, her days and years are happy indeed. And she can look back without a sigh to those days of gloom, which we have endeavoured to describe. *Hic Hymæneus est*—and thus we leave them in their far-off retreat, basking in the golden sunshine of their love.

THE END.

# SAMUEL TINSLEY'S

# PUBLICATIONS.

London:

## SAMUEL TINSLEY,

### 10, SOUTHAMPTON STREET, STRAND.

*.* *Totally distinct from any other firm of Publishers.*

# NOTICE.

# SAMUEL TINSLEY'S
# NEW PUBLICATIONS.

---

## THE POPULAR NEW NOVELS, AT ALL LIBRARIES IN TOWN AND COUNTRY.

---

A DESPERATE CHARACTER: a Tale of the Gold Fever. By W. THOMSON-GREGG. 3 vols., 31s. 6d.

" A novel which cannot fail to interest."—*Daily News.*

ANNALS of the TWENTY-NINTH CENTURY; or, the Autobiography of the Tenth President of the World-Republic. 3 vols., 31s. 6d.

" From beginning to end the book is one long catalogue of wonders. . . . Very amusing, and will doubtless create some little sensation."—*Scotsman.*

"By mere force of originality will more than hold its own among the rank and file of fiction."—*Examiner.*

" Here is a work in certain respects one of the most singular in modern literature, which surpasses all of its class in bold and luxuriant imagination, in vivid descriptive power, in startling—not to say extravagant suggestions —in lofty and delicate moral sympathies. It is difficult to read it with a serious countenance : yet it is impossible not to read it with curious interest, and sometimes with profound admiration. The author's imagination hath run mad, but often there is more in his philosophy than the world may dream of. . . . . We have read his work with almost equal feelings of pleasure, wonderment, and amusement, and this, we think, will be the feelings of most of its readers. On the whole, it is a book of remarkable novelty and unquestionable genius."—*Nonconformist.*

"The adventures of President Milton . . . are told with excellent spirit. The vivid imagination of the author, and his serious and quaint narrative style, are not the only delightful features of this thoroughly amusing book." —*Public Opinion.*

AS THE FATES WOULD HAVE IT. By G. BERESFORD FITZGERALD. Crown 8vo., 10s. 6d.

ALDEN OF ALDENHOLME. By GEORGE SMITH. 3 vols., 31s. 6d.

" Pure and graceful. . . . . Above the average."—*Athenæum.*

BARBARA'S WARNING. By the Author of " Recommended to Mercy." 3 vols., 31s. 6d.

BETWEEN TWO LOVES. By ROBERT J. GRIFFITHS, LL.D. 3 vols., 31s. 6d.

---

Samuel Tinsley, 10, Southampton Street, Strand.

BORN TO BE A LADY.   By KATHERINE HEN-
DERSON.   Crown 8vo., 7s. 6d.

"Miss Henderson has written a really interesting story. . . . The heroine,
Jeanie Monroe, is just what a Jeanie should be—'bonny,' 'sonsie,' 'douce,'
and 'eident,'—having a fair and sound mind in a fair and sound body ;
loving and loyal, true to earthly love, and firm to heavenly faith.   The
novelist's art is exhibited by marrying this gardener's daughter to a man
of shifting principles, higher in a sense than she in the social scale. . . .
The 'local colouring' is excellent, and the subordinate characters, Jeanie's
father especially, capital studies."—*Athenæum.*

BUILDING UPON SAND.   By ELIZABETH J.
LYSAGHT.   Crown 8vo., 10s. 6d.

"It is an eminently lady-like story, and pleasantly told.  .  .  .  .  We
can safely recommend 'Building upon Sand.'"—*Graphic.*

CHASTE AS ICE, PURE AS SNOW.   By Mrs.
M. C. DESPARD.   3 vols., 31s. 6d.   Second Edition.

"A novel of something more than ordinary promise."—*Graphic.*

CRUEL   CONSTANCY.   By KATHARINE KING,
Author of 'The Queen of the Regiment.'   3 vols., 31s. 6d.

"It is a very readable novel, and contains much pleasant writing."—*Pall
Mall Gazette.*

"In this story Miss King has made an advance.   She has avoided many
of the faults which are so apparent in ' Lost for Gold,' and she has bestowed
much pains upon delineation of character and descriptions of Irish life.
Her book possesses originality."—*Morning Post.*

DISINTERRED.   From the Boke of a Monk of
Carden Abbey.   By T. ESMONDE.   Crown 8vo., 7s. 6d.

DR. MIDDLETON'S DAUGHTER.   By the Author
of "A Desperate Character."   3 vols., 31s. 6d.

FAIR, BUT NOT WISE.   By Mrs. FORREST-GRANT.
2 vols., 21s.

"'Fair but not Wise' possesses considerable merit, and is both cleverly
and powerfully written.   If earnest, it is yet amusing and sometimes
humorous, and the interest is well sustained from the first to the last
page."—*Court Express.*

FIRST AND LAST.   By F. VERNON-WHITE. 2 vols.,
21s.

FLORENCE ; or, Loyal Quand Même.   By FRANCES
ARMSTRONG.   Crown 8vo., 5s., cloth.   Post free.

"It is impossible not be interested in the story from beginning to end."
—*Examiner.*

"A very charming love story, eminently pure and lady-like in tone, effective and interesting in plot, and, rarest praise of all, written in excellent English."—*Civil Service Review.*

"The book is excellently printed and nicely bound—in fact it is one which authoress, publisher, and reader may alike regard with mingled satisfaction and pleasure."—*Nottingham Daily Guardian.*

" 'Florence' is readable, even interesting in every part."—*The Scotsman.*

## FOLLATON PRIORY. 2 vols., 21s.

" 'Follaton Priory' is a thoroughly sensational story, written with more art than is usual in compositions of its class ; and avoiding, skilfully, a melancholy termination."—*Sunday Times.*

## GAUNT ABBEY. By ELIZABETH J. LYSAGHT, Author of "Building upon Sand," "Nearer and Dearer," etc. 3 vols., 31s. 6d.

## GOLDEN MEMORIES. By EFFIE LEIGH. 2 vols., 21s.

"There is not a dull page in the book."—*Morning Post.*

## GRAYWORTH: a Story of Country Life. By CAREY HAZELWOOD. 3 vols., 31s. 6d.

"Carey Hazelwood can write well."—*Examiner.*

"Many traces of good feeling and good taste, little touches of quiet humour, denoting kindly observation, and a genuine love of the country."—*Standard.*

## HILLESDEN ON THE MOORS. By ROSA MAC-KENZIE KETTLE, Author of "The Mistress of Langdale Hall." 2 vols., 21s.

"Thoroughly enjoyable, full of pleasant thoughts gracefully expressed, and eminently pure in tone."—*Public Opinion.*

## IN SECRET PLACES. By ROBERT J. GRIFFITHS, LL.D. 3 vols., 31s. 6d.

## IS IT FOR EVER ? By KATE MAINWARING. 3 vols., 31s. 6d.

"A work to be recommended. . . . . A thrillingly sensational novel."—*Sunday Times.*

## JOHN FENN'S WIFE. By MARIA LEWIS. Crown 8vo., 7s. 6d.

**K**ITTY'S RIVAL.   By Sydney Mostyn, Author of 'The Surgeon's Secret,' etc.   3 vols., 31s. 6d.

"Essentially dramatic and absorbing. . . . . We have nothing but unqualified praise for 'Kitty's Rival,' which we recommend as a fresh and natural story, full of homely pathos and kindly humour, and written in a style which shows the good sense of the author has been cultivated by the study of the works of the best of English writers."—*Public Opinion.*

**L**ORD CASTLETON'S WARD.   By Mrs. B. R. Green.   3 vols., 31s. 6d.

"This is novel of character as well as of incident, and Mrs. Green has been studious in balancing fairly the two elements which combine to make her work not only interesting but instructive.   The events are pleasingly described, and are of a nature to arrest attention.   They are natural and dramatic, and so arranged as to succeed each other with increasing interest. The plot, without being intricate, is sufficiently involved to create a desire to follow its development and conclusion. . . . Mrs. Green has written a readable story, fresh and bright. . . . It is very readable."—*Public Opinion.*

**M**ARY GRAINGER: A Story.   By George Leigh. 2 vols., 21s.

**N**EARER AND DEARER.   By Elizabeth J. Lysaght, Author of "Building upon Sand." 3 vols., 31s. 6d.

"A capital story. . . very pleasant reading . . . With the exception of George Eliot, there is no other of our lady writers with whom Mrs. Lysaght will not favourably compare."—*Scotsman.*

"We have said the book is readable.   It is more, it is both clever and interesting."—*Sunday Times.*

**N**EGLECTED; a Story of Nursery Education Forty Years Ago.   By Miss Julia Luard.   Crown 8vo., 5s. cloth.

**O**NLY SEA AND SKY.   A Novel.   2 vols., 21s.

**O**VER THE FURZE.   By Rosa M. Kettle, Author of the "Mistress of Langdale Hall," etc.   3 vols., 31s. 6d.

**N**O FATHERLAND.   By Madame Von Oppen. 2 vols., 21s.

**N**OT TO BE BROKEN.   By W. A. Chandler. Crown 8vo., 10s. 6d.

Samuel Tinsley, 10, Southampton Street, Strand.

PERCY LOCKHART. By F. W. BAXTER. 2 vols., 21s.

"A bright, fresh, healthy story. . . . . Eminently readable."—*Standard*.

"The novel altogether deserves praise. It is healthy in tone, interesting in plot and incident, and generally so well written that few persons would be able justly to find fault with it."—*Scotsman*.

RAVENSDALE. By ROBERT THYNNE, Author of "Tom Delany." 3 vols., 31s. 6d.

"A well-told, natural, and wholesome story."—*Standard*.

"No one can deny merit to the writer."—*Saturday Review*.

SHINGLEBOROUGH SOCIETY. 3 vols., 31s. 6d.

SONS OF DIVES. 2 vols., 21s.

"A well-principled and natural story."—*Athenæum*.

STRANDED, BUT NOT LOST. By DOROTHY BROMYARD. 3 vols., 31s. 6d.

THE BARONET'S CROSS. By MARY MEEKE, Author of "Marion's Path through Shadow to Sunshine." 2 vols., 21s.

"A novel suited to the palates of eager consumers of fiction."—*Sunday Times*.

THE D'EYNCOURTS OF FAIRLEIGH. By THOMAS ROWLAND SKEMP. 3 vols., 31s. 6d.

"An exceedingly readable novel, full of various and sustained interest. . . . . The interest is well kept up all through."—*Daily Telegraph*.

THE HEIR OF REDDESMONT. 3 vols., 31s. 6d.

"Full of interest and life."—*Echo*.

THE INSIDIOUS THIEF: a Tale for Humble Folks. By One of Themselves. Crown 8vo., 5s. Second Edition.

THE LOVE THAT LIVED. By Mrs. EILOART, Author of "The Curate's Discipline," "Just a Woman," "Woman's Wrong," &c. 3 vols., 31s. 6d.

THE MAGIC OF LOVE. By Mrs. FORREST-GRANT, Author of "Fair, but not Wise." 3 vols., 31s. 6d.

THE SECRET OF TWO HOUSES. By FANNY FISHER. 2 vols., 21s.

"Thoroughly dramatic."—*Public Opinion.*
"The story is well told."—*Sunday Times.*

THE SEDGEBOROUGH WORLD. By A. FARE-BROTHER. 2 vols., 21s.

"There is no little novelty and a large fund of amusement in 'The Sedgeborough World.'"—*Illustrated London News.*

THE SURGEON'S SECRET. By SYDNEY MOSTYN, Author of "Kitty's Rival," etc. Crown 8vo., 10s. 6d.

"A most exciting novel—the best on our list. It may be fairly recommended as a very extraordinary book."—*John Bull.*

"A stirring drama, with a number of closely connected scenes, in which there are not a few legitimately sensational situations. There are many spirited passages."—*Public Opinion.*

THE THORNTONS OF THORNBURY. By Mrs. HENRY LOWTHER CHERMSIDE. 3 vols., 31s. 6d.

THE TRUE STORY OF HUGH NOBLE'S FLIGHT. By the Authoress of "What Her Face Said." 10s. 6d.

"A pleasant story, with touches of exquisite pathos, well told by one who is master of an excellent and sprightly style."—*Standard.*

"An unpretending, yet very pathetic story. . . . We can congratulate the author on having achieved a signal success."—*Graphic.*

TIMOTHY CRIPPLE; or, "Life's a Feast." By THOMAS AURIOL ROBINSON. 2 vols., 21s.

"This is a most amusing book, and the author deserves great credit for the novelty of his design, and the quaint humour with which it is worked out."—*Public Opinion.*

"For abundance of humour, variety of incident, and idiomatic vigour of expression, Mr. Robinson deserves, and will no doubt receive, great credit."—*Civil Service Review.*

TOO LIGHTLY BROKEN. 3 vols., 31s. 6d.

"A very pleasing story . . . . . very prettily told."—*Morning Post.*

Samuel Tinsley, 10, Southampton Street, Strand.

TOM DELANY. By ROBERT THYNNE, Author of "Ravensdale." 3 vols., 31s. 6d.

"A very bright, healthy, simply-told story."—*Standard*.

"All the individuals whom the reader meets at the gold-fields are well-drawn, amongst whom not the least interesting is 'Terrible Mac.'"—*Hour*.

"There is not a dull page in the book."—*Scotsman*.

TOWER HALLOWDEANE. 2 vols., 21s.

TWIXT CUP and LIP. By MARY LOVETT-CAMERON. 3 vols., 31s. 6d.

"Displays signs of more than ordinary promise. . . . As a whole the novel cannot fail to please. Its plot is one that will arrest attention; and its characters, one and all, are full of life and have that nameless charm which at once attracts and retains the sympathy of the reader."—*Daily News*.

WAGES: a Story in Three Books. 3 vols., 31s. 6d.

"A work of no commonplace character."—*Sunday Times*.

WANDERING FIRES. By Mrs. M. C. DESPARD, Author of "Chaste as Ice," &c. 3 vols., 31s. 6d.

WEBS OF LOVE. (I. A Lawyer's Device. II. Sancta Simplicitas.) By G. E. H. 1 vol., Crown 8vo., 10s. 6d.

WEIMAR'S TRUST. By Mrs. EDWARD CHRISTIAN. 3 vols., 31s. 6d.

"A novel which deserves to be read, and which, once begun, will not be readily laid aside till the end."—*Scotsman*.

WILL SHE BEAR IT? A Tale of the Weald. 3 vols., 31s. 6d.

"This is a clever story, easily and naturally told, and the reader's interest sustained throughout. . . . A pleasant, readable book, such as we can heartily recommend as likely to do good service in the dull and foggy days before us."—*Spectator*.

"Written with simplicity, good feeling, and good sense, and marked throughout by a high moral tone, which is all the more powerful from never being obtrusive. . . . The interest is kept up with increasing power to the last."—*Standard*.

NOTICE.—Miss **Rosa M.** Kettle's **New Story.**

OVER THE FURZE. By ROSA MACKENZIE KETTLE.
3 vols., 31s. 6d.

*(From the PALL MALL GAZETTE, June 13th, 1874.)*

This pleasantly-written story will be read with enjoyment by many people, especially young people, who are sure to admire the hero. He is, as Thackeray says of Scott's heroes, "handsome, brave, amiable, and not too clever," just the sort of person to charm a very young girl. Other characters in the book have, however, far more distinctness and life than Victor O'Ruark. The authoress has laid her story in the end of the last century, making the French attacks on Ireland the turning events of the book, and introducing us to a group of French refugees, Louis XVIII. among them, and of enthusiastic Irish patriots of good family and gentle manners. There is plenty of stirring incident in the story, which is decidedly above the average; and the way in which it is introduced and told by the nun, who remembers it as connected with her own childhood, is most happy. Mdme. de Luneville, the intriguing Canoness de Rémiremont, is very well sketched, and old Ralph Durham, the gamekeeper, with his bright young wife, stands very clearly before us. But the best sustained character in the book, to our mind, is Lady Mostyn, of old Irish family. The independence of Ireland is the passion of her life, the object for which she economizes, and to which she willingly devotes even the nephew whom she loves best in the world. For her daughter she cares little, save as a possible bride for her beloved nephew, who is to lead the Irish rising in Connemara. A paralytic attack, brought on by anxiety, spares her a part of the pain of his defeat and banishment. Her daughter's devoted nursing softens her by degrees, and she lives to see the marriage which she had long desired. Irish patriotism in those days meant something very different from Fenianism. The old Catholic families were so closely connected with the French Court as to have gained much of its polish; and the stirring events of this half-historical novel are graced by a pleasant setting of rustling silks and old china, and the courtly manners of the *émigrés* of the *ancien régime*.

*(From the SCOTSMAN, June 19th, 1874.)*

As a piece of literary workmanship, "Over the Furze" must be ranked higher than any of Miss Kettle's previous efforts; and in a time when clever writers of fiction are numerous, and when a book must possess exceptional merit to be remarkable, it is entitled to recognition as a novel of undoubted originality and considerable excellence. . . . The book is, on the whole, one which contains much genuinely good work, and will materially add to the author's reputation.

Samuel Tinsley, 10, Southampton Street, Strand.

## Notice:

NEW SYSTEM OF PUBLISHING ORIGINAL NOVELS.

### Vol. I.

THE MISTRESS OF LANGDALE HALL: a Romance of the West Riding. By ROSA MACKENZIE KETTLE. Complete in one handsome volume, with Frontispiece and Vignette by PERCIVAL SKELTON. 4s., post free.

*(From THE SATURDAY REVIEW.)*

Generally speaking, in criticising a novel we confine our observations to the merits of the author. In this case we must make an exception, and say something as to the publisher. The *Mistress of Langdale Hall* does not come before us in the stereotyped three-volume shape, with rambling type, ample margins, and nominally a guinea and a half to pay. On the contrary, this new aspirant to public admiration appears in the modest guise of a single graceful volume, and we confess that we are disposed to give a kindly welcome to the author, because we may flatter ourselves that she is in some measure a *protégée* of our own. A few weeks ago an article appeared in our columns censuring the prevailing fashion of publishing novels at nominal and fancy prices. Necessarily, we dealt a good deal in commonplaces, the absurdity of the fashion being so obvious. We explained, what is well known to every one interested in the matter, that the regulation price is purely illusory. The publisher in reality has to drive his own bargain with the libraries, who naturally beat him down. The author suffers, the trade suffers, and the libraries do not gain. Arguing that a palpable absurdity must be exploded some day unless all the world is qualified for Bedlam, we felt ourselves on tolerably safe ground when we ventured to predict an approaching revolution. Judging from the preface to this book, we may conjecture that it was partly on our hint that Mr. Tinsley has published. As all prophets must welcome events that tend to the speedy accomplishment of their predictions, we confess ourselves gratified by the promptitude with which Mr. Tinsley has acted, and we heartily wish his venture success. He recognises that a reformation so radical must be a work of time, and at first may possibly seem to defeat its object. For it is plain that the public must first be converted to a proper regard for its own interest ; and, by changing the borrowing for the buying system, must come in to buy the publisher out. He must look, moreover, to the support and imitation of his brethren of the trade. We doubt not he has made the venture after all due deliberation, and that we may rely on his determination seconding his enterprise. All prospectuses of new undertakings tend naturally to exaggeration, but success will be well worth the waiting for, should it be only the shadow of that on which Mr. Tinsley reckons. He gives some surprising figures ; he states some startling facts ; and, as a practical man, he draws some practical conclusions. He quotes a statement of Mr. Charles Reade's, to the effect that three publishers in the United States had disposed of no less than 370,000 copies of Mr. Reade's latest novel. He estimates that the profits on that sale—the book being published at a dollar—must amount to £25,000. Mr. Reade, of course, has a name, and we can conceive that his faults and blemishes may positively recommend themselves to American taste. But Mr. Tinsley remarks that if a publisher could sell 70,000 copies in any case, there would still be £5,000 of clear gain ; and even if the new system had a much more moderate success than that, all parties would still profit amazingly. For Mr. Tinsley calculates the profits of a sale of 2,000 copies of a three volume edition at £1,000; and we should fancy the experience of most authors would lead them to believe he overstates it. It will be seen that at all events the new speculation promises brilliantly, and reason and common-sense conspire to tell us that the reward must come to him who has patience to wait. *Palmam qui meruit ferat*, and may he have his share of the profits too. Meanwhile, here we have the first volume of Mr. Tinsley's new series in most legible type, in portable form, and with a sufficiently attractive exterior. The price is four shillings, and, the customary trade deduction being made to circulating libraries, it leaves them without excuse should they deny it to the order of their customers.

We should apologise to Miss Kettle for keeping her waiting while we discuss business matters with her publisher. But she knows, no doubt, that there are times when business must take precedence of pleasure, and conscientious readers are bound to dispose of the preface before proceeding to the book. For we may say at once that we have found pleasure in reading her story. In the first place, it has a strong and natural local colouring, and we always like anything that gives a book individuality. In the next, there is a feminine grace about her pictures of nature and delineations of female character, and that always makes a story attractive. Finally, there is a certain interest that carries us along, although the story is loosely put together, and the demands on our credulity are somewhat incessant and importunate. The scene is laid in the West Riding of Yorkshire ; nor did it need the dedication of the book to tell us that the author was an old resident in the county. With considerable artistic subtlety she lays her scenes in the very confines of busy life. Cockneys and professional foreign tourists are much in the way of believing that the manufacturing districts are severed from the genuinely rural ones by a hard-and-fast line ; that the demons of cotton, coal, and wool blight everything within the scope of their baleful influence. There can be no greater blunder ; native intelligence might tell us that mills naturally follow water power, and that a broad stream and a good fall generally imply wooded banks and sequestered ravines, swirling pools, and rushing rapids. Miss Kettle, as a dweller in the populous and flourishing West Riding, has learned all that, of course. She is aware besides of the power of contrast ; that peace and solitude are never so much appreciated as when you have just quitted the bustle of life, and hear its hum mellowed by the distance. Romance is never so romantic as when it rubs shoulders with the practical, and sensation 'piles itself up' when it is evolved in the centre of common-place life.  .  .  .  .  .  .

The story is interesting and very pleasantly written, and for the sake of both author and publisher we cordially wish it the reception it deserves.

---

## VOL. II.

PUTTYPUT'S PROTÉGÉE ; or, Road, Rail, and River. A Story in Three Books. By HENRY GEORGE CHURCHILL. Crown 8vo., (uniform with " The Mistress of Langdale Hall"), with 14 illustrations by WALLIS MACKAY. Post free, 4s. Second edition.

"It is a lengthened and diversified farce, full of screaming fun and comic delineation—a reflection of Dickens, Mrs. Malaprop, and Mr. Boucicault, and dealing with various descriptions of social life. We have read and laughed, pooh-poohed, and read again, ashamed of our interest, but our interest has been too strong for our shame. Readers may do worse than surrender themselves to its melo-dramatic enjoyment. From title-page to colophon, only Dominie Sampson's epithet can describe it—it is 'prodigious.'"—*British Quarterly Review.*

"It is impossible to read 'Puttyput's Protégée' without being reminded at every turn of the contemporary stage, and the impression it leaves on the mind is very similar to that produced by witnessing a whole evening's entertainment at one of our popular theatres."—*Echo.*

### Samuel Tinsley, 10, Southampton Street, Strand.

EPITAPHIANA; or, the Curiosities of Churchyard
Literature : being a Miscellaneous Collection of Epitaphs,
with an INTRODUCTION. By W. FAIRLEY. Crown 8vo.,
cloth, price 5s. Post free.

"An amusing book. . . . A capital collection of epitaphs."—*Court Circular*.

"Mr. Fairley's industry has been rewarded by an assemblage of grotesque and fantastic epitaphs, such as we never remember to have seen equalled. They fill an elegantly printed volume."—*Cork Examiner*.

"Although we have picked several plums from Mr. Fairley's book, we can assure our readers that there are plenty more left. And now that the long evenings are once more stealing upon us, and the fireside begins to be comfortable, suggesting a book and a quiet read, let us recommend Mr. Fairley, who comes before us in the handsome guise and the capital type of the enterprising Mr. Samuel Tinsley."—*Derbyshire Advertiser*.

HARRY'S BIG BOOTS : a Fairy Tale, for "Smalle
Folke." By S. E. GAY. With 8 Full-page Illustrations
and a Vignette by the author, drawn on wood by PERCIVAL
SKELTON. Crown 8vo., handsomely bound in cloth, price 5s.

"'Harry's Big Boots' is sure of a large and appreciative audience. It is as good as a Christmas pantomime, and its illustrations are quite equal to any transformation scene. . . . The pictures of Harry and Harry's seven-leagued boots, with their little wings and funny faces, leave nothing to be desired."—*Daily News*.

"Some capital fun will be found in 'Harry's Big Boots.'. . . The illustrations are excellent, and so is the story."—*Pall Mall Gazette*.

MOVING EARS. By the Ven. Archdeacon WEAKHEAD,
Rector of Newtown, Kent. 1 vol., crown 8vo., 5s.

A TRUE FLEMISH STORY.    By the Author of
"The Eve of St. Nicholas." In wrapper, 1s.

THE PHYSIOLOGY OF THE SECTS. Crown
8vo., price 5s.

ANOTHER WORLD; or, Fragments from the Star
City of Montalluyah. By HERMES. Third Edition, revised, with additions. Post 8vo., price 12s.

THE FALL OF MAN : An Answer to Mr. Darwin's
"Descent of Man ;" being a Complete Refutation, by
common-sense arguments, of the Theory of Natural Selection.
1s., sewed.

## POETRY, ETC.

MISPLACED LOVE. A Tale of Love, Sin, Sorrow, and Remorse. 1 vol., crown 8vo., 5s.

THE SOUL SPEAKS, and other Poems. By FRANCIS H. HEMERY. In wrapper, 1s.

SUMMER SHADE AND WINTER SUNSHINE: Poems. By ROSA MACKENZIE KETTLE, Author of " The Mistress of Langdale Hall." New Edition. 2s. 6d., cloth.

THE WITCH of NEMI, and other Poems. By EDWARD BRENNAN. Crown 8vo., 10s. 6d.

MARY DESMOND, AND OTHER POEMS. By NICHOLAS J. GANNON. Fcp. 8vo., 4s., cloth. Second Edition.

THE GOLDEN PATH: a Poem. By ISABELLA STUART. 6d., sewed.

THE REDBREAST OF CANTERBURY CATHE-DRAL : Lines from the Latin of Peter du Moulin, some-time a Prebendary of Canterbury. Translated by the Rev. F. B. WELLS, M.A., Rector of Woodchurch. Handsomely bound, price 1s.

THE TICHBORNE AND ORTON AUTOGRAPHS; comprising Autograph Letters of Roger Tichborne, Arthur Orton (to Mary Ann Loder), and the Defendant (early letters to Lady Tichborne, &c.), in facsimile. In wrapper, price 6d.

BALAK AND BALAAM IN EUROPEAN COS-TUME. By the Rev. JAMES KEAN, M.A., Assistant to the Incumbent of Markinch, Fife. 6d., sewed.

ANOTHER ROW AT DAME EUROPA'S SCHOOL. Showing how John's Cook made an IRISH STEW, and what came of it. 6d., sewed.

NOTICE.—A new work by the Hon. Grantley F. Berkeley.

# FACT AGAINST FICTION. The Habits and Treatment of Animals Practically Considered. Hydrophobia and Distemper. With some remarks on Darwin. By the HON. GRANTLEY F. BERKELEY. 2 vols., 8vo., 30s.

*(From the STANDARD, June 8th, 1874.)*

The godson of George the Fourth gives us here two rattling volumes, brimming with egotism, dogmatism, and aggressiveness, all to be forgiven, perhaps, because their author is a veteran, possessing real mastership of his subject, and one who writes from long and diversified experience. All relating to hounds, foxes, horses, birds, wild fowl, fishes, game preserving, and poaching, comes by turn under his hand, and he never flinches from pronouncing an opinion. .... After reading these pages, full of dash and sparkle as they are, we might imagine for a moment that the hunter and the hound were two among the most important elements. It is evident that he has bestowed a patient and intelligent study on the maladies to which they are liable, though all his theories with reference to hydrophobia and rabies may not pass unchallenged. In "dog-reason" he implicitly believes, and illustrates his belief by a great number of illustrations, and he even claims for the animal a "soul."

*(From the PALL MALL GAZETTE, June 17th, 1874.)*

It is refreshing to meet with a book like Mr. Berkeley's, written not only by a sportsman, but by a sportsman of the old school. . . . Taking his volumes all in all, they are an agreeable and useful contribution to a subject which he has studied with all his heart and soul through a long and active lifetime. . . . But for more detailed information on that and many other subjects, we must refer our readers to the volumes, in which they will find very little system, but "a great deal of fine confused feeding," as the Scotchman said of the sheep's head.

*(From the MORNING POST, June 22nd, 1874.)*

A book on field sports and the best means of enjoying them is sometimes as repulsive and dry reading as a work on geometry. Mr. Berkeley here gives an autobiography as much as a hand-book of sports, and intersperses the details of hunting, riding to hounds, and other rural pastimes with so much light and interesting matter that he has provided a consolidated fund of enjoyment for all who take an interest in any branch of rural life. The precepts are thus inculcated in so pleasing a manner and with so many new anecdotes, that the reader unconsciously accepts the opinions thus gracefully insinuated, and rises from the perusal in doubt whether more to admire the sagacity of the veteran author, or the many amiable qualities of his heart, which beam forth ever and anon in this account of his dealings with the inferior animals. Like the sunshine in a good picture, his genial smile and mirthful warmth light up each page and lend additional charms to each sportive scene. . . . Mr. Berkeley treats of all important sporting matters from a practical point of view, and in the way which a first-rate but untaught, or rather untechnical, and unprejudiced sportsman would consider them. A perusal of this work, therefore, will form a habit of mind such as the lover of field sports requires. It is like a hygienic or medical work treating of constitutional and hereditary tendencies rather than of the more technical details which belong to the province of the surgeon. It is certainly impossible to rise from any examination, long or short, of the author's lucubrations without becoming a better sportsman and a more experienced lover of the art than when the book was first opened.

Samuel Tinsley, 10, Southampton Street, Strand.

www.ingramcontent.com/pod-product-compliance
Lightning Source LLC
Chambersburg PA
CBHW031344020726
47499CB00005B/1386